DOCTOR DOLITTLE'S
CIRCUS

THE YEARLING DOCTOR DOLITTLE BOOKS:

THE STORY OF DOCTOR DOLITTLE
THE VOYAGES OF DOCTOR DOLITTLE
DOCTOR DOLITTLE'S CIRCUS
DOCTOR DOLITTLE'S CARAVAN
DOCTOR DOLITTLE AND THE GREEN CANARY
DOCTOR DOLITTLE'S POST OFFICE
DOCTOR DOLITTLE'S GARDEN
DOCTOR DOLITTLE IN THE MOON

YEARLING BOOKS/YOUNG YEARLINGS/YEARLING CLASSICS are designed especially to entertain and enlighten young people. Patricia Reilly Giff, consultant to this series, received her bachelor's degree from Marymount College. She holds a master's degree in history from St. John's University, and a Professional Diploma in Reading from Hofstra University. She was a teacher and reading consultant for many years, and is the author of numerous books for young readers.

For a complete listing of all Yearling titles, write to
Dell Readers Service, P.O. Box 1045,
South Holland, IL 60473.

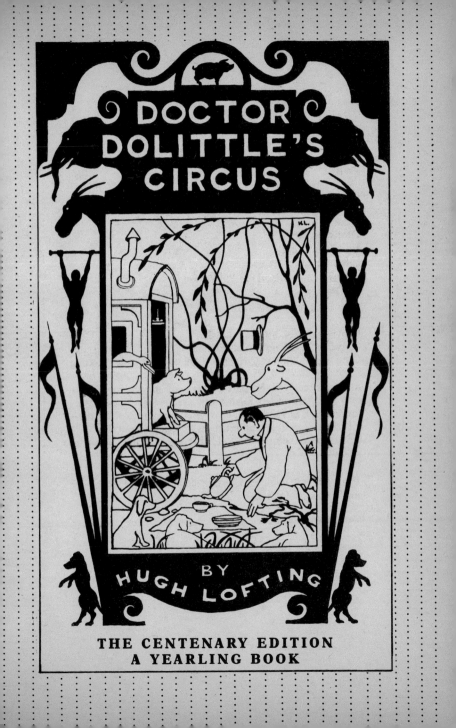

DOCTOR DOLITTLE'S CIRCUS

BY HUGH LOFTING

THE CENTENARY EDITION
A YEARLING BOOK

Published by
Dell Publishing
a division of
Bantam Doubleday Dell Publishing Group, Inc.
666 Fifth Avenue
New York, New York 10103

ISBN: 0-440-40058-9

Printed in the United States of America

July 1988

10 9 8 7 6 5 4 3

CW

· Contents ·

PART ONE

1	The Fireside Circle	3
2	The Doctor Meets a Friend—and a Relative	10
3	Business Arrangements	16
4	The Doctor Is Discovered	23
5	The Doctor Is Discouraged	32
6	Sophie, from Alaska	43
7	The Messenger from the North	48

PART TWO

1	Planning the Escape	59
2	"Animals' Night" at the Circus	71
3	In the Deserted Garden	82
4	The Leader of the Bloodhounds	94
5	The Passengers from Penchurch	107
6	The Grantchester Coach	117

PART THREE

1	The Highwayman's Double	131
2	To the Sea by River	138
3	Sir William Peabody, J. P.	146
4	Nightshade the Vixen	157

PART FOUR

1	Back to the Circus	171
2	The Patent-Medicine Riots	182
3	Nino	190
4	Another Talking Horse	197
5	The Star Gives a Great Performance	204
6	Beppo the Great	211
7	The Perfect Pasture	216
8	The Retired Cab and Wagon Horses' Association	226

PART FIVE

1	Mr. Bellamy of Manchester	237
2	The Poster and the Statue	246
3	Fame, Fortune—and Rain	257
4	Mr. Blossom's Mysterious Disappearance	267
5	The Doctor Becomes Manager of the Circus	273
6	Matthew Mugg, Assistant Manager	278
7	The Dolittle Circus	282
	About the Author	291

· Illustrations ·

"He could crow only in a whisper"   6
" 'Why, it's Matthew Mugg!' "   7
"The Doctor took hold of the bridle"   13
"He waved his sandwich toward the sky"   19
" 'Hooray for the circus!' "   21
"Waiting on the front steps"   24
"One of the marsupials"   28
" 'You leave them snakes alone!' "   30
"Too-Too was always there"   34
"On the scent of a fox"   38
"Toby and Swizzle"   41
"Climbed wearily from his bed"   42
" 'I ought to go to him' "   46
"He crawled under the bed"   51
" 'I don't care that much' "   54
"Swizzle bowed to an imaginary audience"   61
"Made his way through unfrequented streets"   63
"His nimble fingers soon had the door unlocked"   66
" 'Oh! Oh! I'm feeling faint!' "   70
"A small pig tripped him up"   72
"He stamped his floor into kindling wood"   75
"He lowered the ladder into the garden"   81
"The dog took the flying dive"   86
"Sophie smiled"   88
"John Dolittle paused"   92
"A steeplechase over hill and dale"   99
"He found a hole for Sophie to crawl through"   100
" 'Yes,' said the ducks"   103
"He carried her to the coach"   110

" 'How would this do?' "   113

"He put the veil across her face"   115

" 'Excuse me, my dear,' she began"   119

"He heard the voices of two men at a table within"   122

"John Dolittle peered through them"   127

"He rigged up a kind of harness"   134

"Came marching back with the scarecrow on his shoulder"   135

"They reached Hobbs's Mill just as evening was coming on"   141

"He threw Sophie into the Bristol Channel"   144

" 'You Bluebeard!' "   148

"He found a badly made 'M. M.' "   150

" 'Excellent bread you have here' "   155

"He came to a crossroads"   159

" 'It's a case of flat feet' "   162

"Sir William turned and drew rein"   166

"All yapping about the foot of an oak tree"   173

" 'They hated it,' the snake said"   176

" 'I'll slap your face' "   185

" 'He's bought six fat snakes with it!' "   188

"They had made their usual procession through the streets"   191

" 'You can't have this horse perform today' "   196

" 'Why, Doctor, how can you say such a thing?' "   201

" 'Listen, Hop!' "   205

" 'The Commander-in-Chief of the Russian Army' "   209

"He had handbills given away in the streets"   215

"Massaging the elephant"   217

"The old plow horse was introduced to Beppo"   221

"They looked over a wide farm gate"   223

"John Dolittle knocked upon his door"   227

" 'Would you like to earn a shilling a week?' "   231

" 'What's the use?' cried Too-Too"   233

"It was a part of the life Gub-Gub greatly enjoyed"   240

"The pantomime was performed by the side of the road"   243

"He would arrive on the stage wearing only a coat
    and a wig"   245

ILLUSTRATIONS

"He set out to see the sights of Manchester" 249

"The footman came out and pushed big cards into them" 252

"Gub-Gub used to practice it by the hour" 255

"Dab-Dab curtsied like a regular ballerina" 259

"Gub-Gub handing around cakes" 263

"The Pinto brothers arrived" 270

" 'But I don't know anything about circus management!' " 274

"Putting up the new sign" 277

"Free packets of peppermints for the children" 281

"The snakes' quadrille" 288

I would like to acknowledge the following editors whose faith in the literary value of these children's classics was invaluable in the publication of the new editions: Janet Chenery, consulting editor; Olga Fricker, Hugh Lofting's sister-in-law, who worked closely with the author and edited the last four original books; Lori Mack, associate editor at Dell; and Lois Myller, whose special love for Doctor Dolittle helped make this project possible.

CHRISTOPHER LOFTING

PART I

· The First Chapter ·

THE FIRESIDE CIRCLE

HIS is the story of that part of Doctor Dolittle's adventures which came about through his joining and traveling with a circus. The Dolittle party, Jip the dog, Dab-Dab the duck, Too-Too the owl, Gub-Gub the pig, the pushmi-pullyu (the extraordinary two-headed animal that the doctor had brought back with him from Africa), and the white mouse, had returned at last to the little house in Puddleby-on-the-Marsh after their long journey from Africa. It was a large family to find food for. And the Doctor, without a penny in his pockets, had been worried over how he was going to feed it. However, the thoughtful Dab-Dab had made them carry up from the ship such supplies as remained in the larder after the voyage was done. These, she said, should last the household—with economy—for a day or two at least.

The animals' delight on getting back home had banished every care or thought of the morrow from the minds of all —except Dab-Dab. That good housekeeper had gone straight to the kitchen and set about the cleaning of pots and the cooking of food. The rest of them, the Doctor included, had gone out into the garden to reexplore all the well-known spots. And they were still roaming and poking around every nook and corner of their beloved home when they were suddenly summoned to luncheon by Dab-Dab's dinner bell —a frying pan beaten with a spoon. At this there was a grand rush for the back door. And they all came trundling in from the garden, gabbling with delight at the prospect of taking a meal again in the dear old kitchen where they had in times past spent so many jolly hours together.

"It will be cold enough for a fire tonight," said Jip as they took their places at the table. "This September wind has a chilly snap in it. Will you tell us a story after supper, Doctor? It's a long time since we sat around the hearth in a ring."

"Or read to us out of your animal storybooks," said Gub-Gub, "the one about the fox who tried to steal the King's goose."

"Well, maybe," said the Doctor. "We'll see. We'll see. What delicious sardines these are! From Bordeaux, by the taste of them. There's no mistaking real French sardines."

At this moment the Doctor was called away to see a patient in the surgery—a weasel who had broken a claw. And he was no sooner done with that when a rooster with a sore throat turned up from a neighboring farm. He was so hoarse, he said, he could crow only in a whisper, and nobody on his farm woke up in the morning. Then two pheasants arrived to show him a scrawny chick that had never been able to peck properly since it was born.

For, although the people in Puddleby had not yet learned of the Doctor's arrival, news of his coming had already spread among the animals and the birds. And all that afternoon he was kept busy bandaging, advising, and giving out doses of medicine, while a huge motley crowd of creatures waited patiently outside the surgery door.

"Ah me!—just like old times," sighed Dab-Dab. "No peace. Patients clamoring to see him morning, noon, and night."

Jip had been right: by the time darkness came that night it was very chilly. Wood enough was found in the cellar to start a jolly fire in the big chimney. Round this the animals gathered after supper and pestered the Doctor for a story or a chapter from one of his books.

"But look here," said he. "What about the circus?"

During his recent African voyage, the Doctor had borrowed a sailor's boat. Unfortunately, the boat was wrecked, but Doctor Dolittle was persuaded by his animal friends to bring back that rarest of animals, the pushmi-pullyu. The animals' idea was that they would join a circus and put the pushmi-pullyu on display. By that means, the Doctor could earn enough money to pay the sailor for his boat, and even have some money left over for his own household.

"If we're going to make money to pay the sailor back we've got to be thinking of that. We haven't even found a circus to go with yet. I wonder what's the best way to set about it. They travel all over the place, you know. Let me see: who could I ask?"

"Sh!" said Too-Too. "Wasn't that the front doorbell ringing?"

"Strange!" said the Doctor, getting up from his chair. "Callers already?"

When John Dolittle had lit the candles in the hall he opened the front door. And there standing on the threshold was the cat's-meat man.

"Why, it's Matthew Mugg, as I'm alive!" he cried. "Come in Matthew, come in. But how did you know I was here?"

"I felt it in my bones, Doctor," said the cat's-meat man,

"He could crow only in a whisper"

stumping into the hall. "Only this morning I says to my wife, 'Theodosia,' I says, 'something tells me the Doctor's got back. And I'm going up to his house tonight to take a look.'"

"Well, I'm glad to see you," said John Dolittle. "Let's go into the kitchen where it's warm."

Although he said he had only come on the chance of finding the Doctor, the cat's-meat man had brought presents with him: a knucklebone off a shoulder of mutton for Jip; a piece of cheese for the white mouse; a turnip for Gub-Gub and a pot of flowering geraniums for the Doctor. When the visitor was comfortably settled in the armchair before the

" 'Why, it's Matthew Mugg!' "

fire John Dolittle handed him the tobacco jar from the mantelpiece and told him to fill his pipe.

"I got your letter about the sparrow," said Matthew. "He found you all right, I s'pose."

"Yes, and he was very useful to me. He left the ship when we were off the Devon coast. He was anxious to get back to London."

"Are you home for a long stay now?"

"Well—yes and no," said the Doctor. "I'd like nothing better than to enjoy a few quiet months here and get my garden to rights. It's in a shocking mess. But unfortunately I've got to make some money first."

"Humph," said Matthew, puffing at his pipe. "Meself, I've bin trying to do that all my life. Never was very good at it. But I've got twenty-five shillings saved up, if that would help you."

"It's very kind of you, Matthew, very. The fact is I—er—I need a whole lot of money. I've got to pay back some debts. But listen: I have a strange kind of new animal—a pushmi-pullyu. He has two heads. The monkeys in Africa presented him to me after I had cured an epidemic for them. Their idea was that I should travel with him in a circus—on show, you know. Would you like to see him?"

"I surely would," said the cat's-meat man. "Sounds like something very new."

"He's out in the garden," said the Doctor. "Don't stare at him too hard. He isn't used to it yet. Gets frightfully embarrassed. Let's take a bucket of water with us and just pretend we've brought him a drink."

When Matthew came back into the kitchen with the Doctor he was all smiles and enthusiasm.

"Why, John Dolittle," said he, "you'll make your fortune—sure as you're alive! There's never bin anything seen like that since the world began. And anyway, I always thought you ought to go into the circus business—you, the only man living that knows animal language. When are you going to start?"

"That's just the point. Perhaps you can help me. I'd want to be sure it was a nice circus I was going with—people I would like, you understand."

Matthew Mugg bent forward and tapped the Doctor on the knee with the stem of his pipe.

"I know the very concern you want," said he. "Right now

over at Grimbledon there's the nicest little circus you ever saw. Grimbledon Fair's on this week and they'll be there till Saturday. Me and Theodosia saw 'em the first day they was on. It isn't a large circus but it's a good one—select like. What do you say if I take you over there tomorrow and you have a chat with the ringmaster?"

"Why that would be splendid," said the Doctor. "But in the meantime don't say anything to anyone about the idea at all. We must keep the pushmi-pullyu a secret till he is actually put on show before the public."

· The Second Chapter ·

THE DOCTOR MEETS A FRIEND— AND A RELATIVE

NOW, Matthew Mugg was a peculiar man. He loved trying new jobs—which was one reason, perhaps, that he never made much money. But his attempts to get into some new kind of work usually ended in his coming back to selling cat's meat and rat-catching for farmers and millers around Puddleby.

Matthew had already at Grimbledon Fair tried to get a job with the circus and been refused. But now that he found the Doctor was going into the business—and with such a wonderful exhibition as a pushmi-pullyu—his hopes rose again. And as he went home that night he already in imagination saw himself in partnership with his beloved doctor, running the biggest circus on earth.

Next day he called at the little house early. After Dab-Dab had made them up some sardine sandwiches to take with them for lunch, they set out.

It was a long walk from Puddleby to Grimbledon. But after the Doctor and the cat's-meat man had been trudging down the road awhile, they heard a sound of hoofs behind them. They turned around; and there was a farmer coming toward them in a trap. Seeing the two travelers upon the road, the farmer was going to offer them a ride. But his wife did not like the ragged looks of the cat's-meat man, and she forbade her husband to stop for them.

"What d'yer think of that for Christian charity?" said the cat's-meat man as the cart went spinning by them. "Sit comfortable in their seats and leave us to walk! That's Isidore Stiles, the biggest potato-grower in these parts. I often catches rats for him. And his wife, the snobby old scarecrow! Did yer see that look she give me? A rat-catcher ain't good enough company for her!"

"But look," said the Doctor. "They're stopping and turning the trap around."

Now this farmer's horse knew the Doctor very well both by sight and reputation. And as he had trotted by he had recognized the little man tramping along the road as none other than the famous John Dolittle. Delighted to find that his friend had returned to these parts, the horse had then turned around of his own accord, and was now trotting back—in spite of his driver's pulling—to greet the Doctor and inquire about his health.

"Where are you going?" asked the horse as he came up.

"We're going to Grimbledon Fair," said the Doctor.

"So are we," said the horse. "Why don't you get into the back of the trap beside the old woman?"

"They haven't invited me," said the Doctor. "See, your farmer is trying to turn you around again toward Grimbledon. Better not anger him. Run along. Don't bother about us. We'll be all right."

Very unwillingly the horse finally obeyed the driver, turned about, and set off once more for the fair. But he hadn't gone more than half a mile before he said to himself,

It's a shame the great man should have to walk while these bumpkins ride. I'm hanged if I'll leave him behind!

Then he pretended to shy at something in the road, swung the trap around again suddenly, and raced back toward the Doctor at full gallop. The farmer's wife screamed and her husband threw all his weight on the reins. But the horse took not the slightest notice. Reaching the Doctor he started rearing and bucking and carrying on like a wild colt.

"Get into the trap, Doctor," he whispered. "Get in, or I'll spill these boobies into the ditch."

The Doctor, fearing an accident, took hold of the horse's bridle and patted him on the nose. Instantly he became as calm and gentle as a lamb.

"Your horse is a little restive, sir," said the Doctor to the farmer. "Would you let me drive him for a spell? I am a veterinary surgeon."

"Why, certainly," said the farmer. "I thought I knew something about horses meself. But I can't do a thing with him this morning."

Then, as the Doctor climbed up and took the reins, the cat's-meat man got in behind and, chuckling with delight, sat beside the indignant wife.

"Nice day, Mrs. Stiles," said Matthew Mugg. "How are the rats in the barn?"

They reached Grimbledon about the middle of the morning. The town was very full and busy and holidayfied. In the cattle market fine prize pigs, fat sheep, and pedigreed draft horses with ribbons in their manes filled the pens.

Through the good-natured crowds that thronged the streets the Doctor and Matthew made their way patiently toward the enclosure where the circus was. The Doctor began to get worried that he might be asked to pay to go in, because he hadn't a single penny in his pockets. But at the

HUGH LOFTING

"The Doctor took hold of the bridle"

entrance to the circus they found a high platform erected, with some curtains at the back. It was like a small outdoor theater. On this platform a man with an enormous black mustache was standing. From time to time various showily-dressed persons made their appearance through the curtains; and the big man introduced them to the gaping crowd and told of the wonders they could perform. Whatever they were, clowns, acrobats or snake charmers, he always said they were the greatest in the world. The crowd was tremendously impressed; and every once in a while people in ones and twos would make their way through the throng, pay

their money at the little gate, and pass into the circus enclosure.

"There you are," the cat's-meat man whispered in the Doctor's ear. "Didn't I tell yer it was a good show? Look! People
going in by hundreds."

"Is that big man the manager?" asked the Doctor.

"Yes, that's him. That's Blossom himself—Alexander
Blossom. He's the man we've come to see."

The Doctor began to squirm his way forward through the
people, with Matthew following behind. Finally he reached
the front and started making signs to the big man on the
platform above to show that he wanted to speak to him. But
Mr. Blossom was so busy bellowing about the wonders of
his show that the Doctor—a small man in a big crowd—
could not attract his attention.

"Get up on the platform," said Matthew. "Climb up and
talk to him."

So the Doctor clambered up on corner of the stage and
then suddenly got frightfully embarrassed to find himself
facing so large a gathering of people. However, once there,
he plucked up his courage and, tapping the shouting showman on the arm, he said, "Excuse me."

Mr. Blossom stopped roaring about the "greatest show on
earth" and gazed down at the little round man who had
suddenly appeared beside him.

"Er—er—" the Doctor began.

Then there was a silence. The people began to titter.

Blossom, like most showmen, was never at a loss for
words and seldom missed an opportunity of being funny at
somebody else's expense. And while John Dolittle was still
wondering how to begin, the manager suddenly turned to
the crowd again and, waving his arm toward the Doctor,
shouted, "And this, Ladies and Gentlemen, is the original

Humpty-Dumpty—the one what gave the king's men so much trouble. Pay your money and come in! Walk up and see 'im fall off the wall!"

At that the crowd roared with laughter and the poor Doctor got more embarrassed than ever.

"Talk to him, Doctor, *talk* to him!" called the cat's-meat man from down below.

Soon, when the laughter had subsided, the Doctor made another attempt. He had just opened his mouth when a single piercing cry rang from amidst the crowd—*"John!"*

The Doctor turned and gazed over the heads of the people to see who was calling him by name. And there on the outskirts of the throng he saw a woman waving violently to him with a green parasol.

"Who is it?" said the cat's-meat man.

"Heaven preserve us!" groaned the Doctor, shamefacedly climbing down off the stage. "What'll we do now? Matthew —*it's Sarah!*"

· The Third Chapter ·

BUSINESS ARRANGEMENTS

Well, well, Sarah!" said John Dolittle when he had finally made his way to her. "My, how well and plump you're looking!"

"I'm nothing of the sort, John," said Sarah severely. "Will you please tell me what you mean by gallivanting around on that platform like a clown? Wasn't it enough for you to throw away the best practice in the West Country for the sake of pet mice and frogs and things? Have you no pride? What were you doing up there?"

"I was thinking of going into the circus business," said the Doctor.

Sarah gasped and put her hand to her head as though about to swoon. Then a long lean man in parson's clothes who was standing behind her came and took her by the arm.

"What is it, my dear?" said he.

"Launcelot," said Sarah weakly, "this is my brother, John Dolittle. John, this is the Reverend Launcelot Dingle, rector of Grimbledon, my husband. But, John, you can't be serious. Go into the circus business! How disgraceful! You must be joking—and who is the person?" she added as Matthew Mugg shuffled up and joined the party.

"This is Matthew Mugg," said the Doctor. "You remember him, of course?"

"Ugh!—the rat-catcher," said Sarah, closing her eyes in horror.

"Not at all. He's a meat merchant," said the Doctor. "Mr. Mugg, the Reverend Launcelot Dingle." And the Doctor introduced his ragged, greasy friend as if he had been a king. "He's my most prominent patient," he added.

"But listen, John," said Sarah, "if you do go into this mad business, promise me you'll do it under some other name. Think what it would mean to our position here if it got known that the rector's brother-in-law was a common showman!"

The Doctor thought a moment. Then he smiled. "All right, Sarah, I'll use some other name. But I can't help it if someone recognizes me, can I?"

After they had bidden farewell to Sarah, the Doctor and Matthew again sought out the manager. They found him counting money at the gate, and this time were able to talk to him at their ease.

John Dolittle described the wonderful animal that he had at home and said he wanted to join the circus with him. Alexander Blossom admitted he would like to see the creature and told the Doctor to bring him there. But John Dolittle said it would be better and easier if the manager came to Puddleby to look at him.

This was agreed upon. And after they had explained to Blossom how to get to the little house on Oxenthorpe Road, they set out for home again, very pleased with their success so far.

"If you do go with Blossom's circus," Matthew asked, as

they tramped along the road chewing sardine sandwiches, "will you take me with you, Doctor? I'd come in real handy, taking care of the caravan, feeding and cleaning and the likes o' that."

"You're very welcome to come, Matthew," said the Doctor. "But what about your own business?"

"Oh, that," said Matthew, biting viciously into another sandwich. "There ain't no money in that. Besides, it's so tame, handing out bits of meat on skewers to overfed poodles! There's no . . . no what d'y' call it?"—he waved his sandwich toward the sky—"no adventure in it. I'm naturally venturesome—reckless like—always was, from my cradle up. Now the circus: That's real life! That's a man's job."

"But how about your wife?" asked the Doctor.

"Theodosia? Oh, she'd come along. She's venturesome, like me. She could mend the clothes and do odd jobs. What do you think?"

"What do I think?" asked the Doctor, who was staring down at the road as he walked. "I was thinking of Sarah."

"Queer gent, that what she married, ain't he," said Matthew, "the Reverend Dangle?"

"Dingle," the Doctor corrected. "Yes. He's venturesome too. It's a funny world! Poor dear Sarah! Poor old Dingle! Well, well."

Late that night, when the Grimbledon Fair had closed, Mr. Blossom, the ringmaster, came to the Doctor's house in Puddleby.

After he had been shown by the light of a lantern the pushmi-pullyu grazing on the lawn, he came back into the library with the Doctor and said, "How much do you want for that animal?"

"No, no, he's not for sale," said the Doctor.

"Oh, come now," said the manager. "You don't want him.

"He waved his sandwich toward the sky"

Anyone could see you're not a regular showman. I'll give you twenty pounds for him."

"No," said the Doctor.

"Thirty pounds," said Blossom.

Still the Doctor refused.

"Forty pounds—fifty pounds," said the manager. Then he went up and up, offering prices that made the cat's-meat man, who was listening, open his eyes wider and wider with wonder.

"It's no use," said the Doctor at last. "You must either take me with the animal into your circus or leave him where he is. I have promised that I myself will see he is properly treated."

"What do you mean?" asked the showman. "Ain't he your property? Who did you promise?"

"He's his own property," said the Doctor. "He came here to oblige me. It was to himself, the pushmi-pullyu, that I gave my promise."

"What! Are you crazy?" asked the showman. Matthew Mugg was going to explain to Blossom that the Doctor could speak animals' language. But John Dolittle motioned to him to be silent.

"And so, you see," he went on, "you must either take me *and* the animal or neither."

Then Blossom said no, he wouldn't agree to that arrangement. And to Matthew's great disappointment and grief he took his hat and left.

But he had expected the Doctor to change his mind and give in. And he hadn't been gone more than ten minutes before he rang the doorbell and said that he had come back to talk it over.

Well, the upshot of it was that the showman finally consented to all the Doctor asked. The pushmi-pullyu and his party were to be provided with a new wagon all to themselves and, although traveling as part of the circus, were to be entirely free and independent. The money made was to be divided equally between the Doctor and the manager. Whenever the pushmi-pullyu wanted a day off he was to have it, and whatever kind of food he asked for was to be provided by Blossom.

When all the arrangements had been gone into, the man said he would send the caravan there next day, and prepared to go.

" 'Hooray for the circus!' "

"By the way," he said, pausing at the front door. "What's your name?"

The Doctor was just about to tell him, when he remembered Sarah's request.

"Oh, well, call me John Smith," said he.

"All right, Mr. Smith," said the showman. "Have your party ready by eleven in the morning. Good night."

"Good night," said the Doctor.

As soon as the door had closed Dab-Dab, Gub-Gub, Jip, Too-Too, and the white mouse, who had been hiding and listening in various corners of the house, all came out into the hall and started chattering at the top of their voices.

"Hooray!" grunted Gub-Gub. "Hooray for the circus!"

"My," said Matthew to the Doctor, "you're not such a bad businessman after all! You got Blossom to give in to everything. He wasn't going to let the chance slip. Did you see how quickly he came back when he thought the deal was off? I'll bet he expects to make a lot of money out of us."

"Poor old home," sighed Dab-Dab, affectionately dusting off the hat rack. "To leave it again so soon!"

"Hooray—" yelled Gub-Gub, trying to stand on his hind legs and balance the Doctor's hat on his nose. "Hooray for the circus! Tomorrow! *Whee!*"

· The Fourth Chapter ·

THE DOCTOR IS DISCOVERED

VERY early the next morning Dab-Dab had the whole house astir. She said breakfast must be eaten and the table cleared before seven, if everything was to be got in readiness for their departure by eleven.

As a matter of fact, the diligent housekeeper had the house closed and everybody waiting outside on the front steps hours before the wagon arrived. But the Doctor, for one, was still kept busy. For up to the last minute animal patients were still coming in from all parts of the countryside, with various ailments to be cured.

At last Jip, who had been out scouting, came rushing back to the party gathered in the garden.

"The wagon's coming," he panted, ". . . all red and yellow . . . it's just around the bend."

Then everybody got excited and began grabbing parcels. Gub-Gub's luggage was a bundle of turnips, and just as he was hurrying down the steps to the road, the string broke and the round white vegetables went rolling all over the place.

The wagon, when it finally came in sight, was certainly a

23

HUGH LOFTING

"Waiting on the front steps"

thing of beauty. It was made like a Gypsy caravan, with
windows and door and chimney. It was very gayly painted
and quite new.

Not so the horse; he was quite old. The Doctor said that
never had he seen an animal so worn out and weary. He got
into conversation with him and found out that he had been
working in the circus for thirty-five years. He was very sick
of it, he said. His name was Beppo. The Doctor decided he
would tell Blossom that it was high time Beppo should be
pensioned off and allowed to live in peace.

They reached the Grimbledon fairgrounds about two

o'clock in the afternoon and entered the circus enclosure by a back gate. Inside they found the great Blossom himself waiting to welcome them.

He seemed quite surprised, on the van's being opened, to find the odd collection of creatures the Doctor had brought with him—he was particularly astonished at the pig. However, he was so delighted to have the pushmi-pullyu that he didn't mind.

He at once led them to what he called their stand—which, he said, he had had built for them that very morning. This the Doctor found to be similar to the place where he had first spoken with Blossom. It was a platform raised three feet from the ground, so that the board and canvas room on the top of it could be seen. It had steps up to it, and a little way back from the front edge of the platform, curtains covered the entrance to the room, so no one could see inside unless they paid to go in.

Across the front of it was a sign:

THE PUSHMI-PULLYU!
COME AND SEE THE MARVELOUS
TWO-HEADED ANIMAL
FROM THE JUNGLES OF AFRICA!
ADMISSION: SIXPENCE

The red and yellow wagon (in which the Doctor's party, with the exception of the pushmi-pullyu, were to live) was backed behind the "stand." And Dab-Dab immediately set about making up beds and arranging the inside so it would be homelike.

Blossom wanted to have the pushmi-pullyu put on show at once, but the Doctor refused. He said any wild animal would need to rest after the journey from Puddleby. And he wished the timid beast to get used to the noisy bustle of circus life before he was stared at by a crowd of holiday-makers.

Blossom was disappointed, but he had to give in. Then, to the animals' delight, he offered to show the Doctor around the circus and introduce him to the various performers. So after the pushmi-pullyu had been moved to his new home in the stand and the Doctor had seen that he was provided with hay and water and bedding, the Puddleby party started out to make a tour of the circus under the guidance of the great Alexander Blossom, ringmaster.

The main show took place only twice a day (at two in the afternoon and at six-thirty at night), in a big tent in the middle of the enclosure. But all around this there were smaller tents and stands, most of which you had to pay extra to get into. Of these the Doctor's establishment was now to form one. They contained all manner of wonders: shooting galleries, guessing games, wild men of Borneo, bearded ladies, merry-go-rounds, strong men, snake charmers, a menagerie, and many more.

Blossom took the Doctor and his friends to the menagerie first. It was a dingy third-rate sort of collection. Most of the animals seemed dirty and unhappy. The Doctor was so saddened he was all for having a row with Blossom over it. But the cat's-meat man whispered in his ear, "Don't be starting trouble right away, Doctor. Wait awhile. After the boss sees how valuable you are with performing animals, you'll be able to do what you like with him. If you kick up a shindy now, we'll maybe lose our job. Then you won't be able to do anything."

This struck John Dolittle as good advice. And he contented himself for the present with whispering to the animals through the bars of their cages that later he hoped to do something for them.

Just as they had entered, a dirty man was taking around a group of country folk to show them the collection. Stopping before a cage where a small furry animal was imprisoned, the man called out, "And this, ladies and gents, is the famous hurri-gurri, from the forests of Patagonia. 'E 'angs from the trees by 'is tail. Pass on to the next cage."

The Doctor, followed by Gub-Gub, went over and looked in at "the famous hurri-gurri."

"Why," said he, "that's nothing but a common opossum from America. One of the marsupials."

"How do you know it's a ma soupial, Doctor?" asked Gub-Gub. "She hasn't any children with her. Perhaps it's a pa soupial."

"And this," roared the man, standing before the next cage, "is the largest elephant in captivity."

"Almost the smallest one I ever saw," murmured the Doctor.

Then Mr. Blossom suggested that they go on to the next show, Princess Fatima, the snake charmer. And he led the way out of the close, evil-smelling menagerie into the open air. As the Doctor passed down the line of cages he hung his head, frowning unhappily. For the various animals, recognizing the great John Dolittle, were all making signs to him to stop and talk with them.

When they entered the snake charmer's tent there were no other visitors there for the moment but themselves. On the small stage they beheld the Princess Fatima, powdering her large nose and swearing to herself in cockney. Beside her chair was a big shallow box full of snakes. Matthew Mugg peeped into it, gasped with horror, and then started to run from the tent.

"One of the marsupials"

"It's all right, Matthew," the Doctor called out. "Don't be alarmed. They're quite harmless."

"What d'yer mean, harmless?" snorted the Princess Fatima, glaring at the Doctor. "They're king cobras, from India —the deadliest snakes livin'."

"They're nothing of the sort," said the Doctor. "They're American blacksnakes—nonpoisonous." And he tickled one under the chin.

"Leave them snakes alone!" yelled Fatima, rising from her chair—"or I'll knock yer bloomin' 'ead orf."

At this moment Blossom interfered and introduced the ruffled princess to Mr. Smith.

The conversation that followed (Fatima was still too angry to take much part in it) was interrupted by the arrival of some people who had come to see the snake charmer perform. Blossom led the Doctor's party off into a corner, whispering, "She's marvelous, Smith. One of the best turns I've got. Just you watch her."

Behind the curtains at the back somebody started beating a drum and playing a pipe. Then Fatima arose, lifted two snakes out of the box, and wound them around her neck and arms.

"Will ze ladies and ze gentlemen step a little closair," she cooed softly to her audience. "Zen zay can see bettair—zo!"

"What's she talking like that for?" Gub-Gub whispered to the Doctor.

"Sh! I suppose she thinks she's speaking with an Oriental accent," said John Dolittle.

"Sounds to me like a hot-potato accent," muttered Gub-Gub. "Isn't she fat and wobbly!"

Noticing that the Doctor did not seem favorably impressed, the circus master led them out to see the other sideshows.

At the next booth a large audience was gathered and yokels were gasping in wonder as the strong man lifted enormous weights in the air. There was no fake about this show. And John Dolittle, deeply interested, joined in the clapping and the gasping.

The strong man was an honest-looking fellow, with tremendous muscles. The Doctor took a liking to him right away. One of his tricks was to lie on the stage on his back and lift an enormous dumbbell with his feet till his legs were sticking right up in the air. It needed balance as well

" 'You leave them snakes alone!' "

as strength because if the dumbbell should fall the wrong way the man would certainly be injured. Today when he had finally brought his legs into an upright position the crowd was whispering in admiration, suddenly there was a loud crack. One of the boards of the stage had given way. Instantly, down came the big dumbbell right across the man's chest.

The crowd screamed and Blossom jumped up on the platform. It took two men's strength to lift the dumbbell off the strong man's body. But even then he did not arise. He lay motionless, his eyes closed, his face a deathly white.

"Get a doctor," Blossom shouted to the cat's-meat man. "Hurry! He's hurt hisself—unconscious. A doctor, quick!"

But John Dolittle was already on the stage, standing over the ringmaster, who knelt beside the injured man.

"Get out of the way and let me examine him," he said quietly.

"What can you do? He's hurt bad. Look, his breathing's queer. We got to get a doctor."

"I am a doctor," said John Dolittle. "Matthew, run to the van and get my black bag."

"You a doctor!" said Blossom, getting up off his knees. "Thought you called yourself *Mr. Smith.*"

"Of course he's a doctor," came a voice out of the crowd. "There wur a time when he wur the best known doctor in the West Country. I know un. Dolittle's his name—John Dolittle, of Puddleby-on-the-Marsh."

· The Fifth Chapter ·

THE DOCTOR IS DISCOURAGED

THE Doctor found that two of the strong man's ribs had been broken by the dumbbell. However, he prophesied that with so powerful a constitution the patient should recover quickly. The injured man was put to bed in his own caravan and until he was well again the Doctor visited him four times a day and Matthew slept in his wagon to nurse him.

The strong man (his show name was Hercules) was very thankful to John Dolittle and became greatly attached to him—and very useful sometimes, as you will see later on.

So the Doctor felt, when he went to bed that first night of his circus career, that if he had made an enemy in Fatima, the snake charmer, he had gained a friend in Hercules, the strong man.

Of course, now that he had been recognized as the odd physician of Puddleby-on-the-Marsh, there was no longer any sense in his trying to conceal who he was. And very soon he became known among the circus folk as just "the Doctor" or "the Doc." On the very high recommendation of Hercules, he was constantly called upon for the cure of small ailments by everyone, from the bearded lady to the clown.

The next day, the pushmi-pullyu was put on show for the first time. He was very popular. A two-headed animal had never before been seen in a circus and the people thronged up to pay their money and have a look at him. At first he nearly died of embarrassment and shyness, and he was for-ever hiding one of his heads under the straw so as not to have to meet the gaze of all those staring eyes. Then the people wouldn't believe he had more than one head. So the Doctor asked him if he would be so good as to keep both of them in view.

"You need not look at the people," he said. "But just let them see that you really have two heads. You can turn your back on the audience—both ends."

But some of the silly people, even when they could see the two heads plainly, kept saying that one must be faked. And they would prod the poor, timid animal with sticks to see if part of him was stuffed. While two country bumpkins were doing this one day the pushmi-pullyu got annoyed, and bringing both his heads up sharply at the same time, he jabbed the two inquirers in the legs. Then they knew for sure that he was real and alive all over.

But as soon as the cat's-meat man could be spared from nursing Hercules (he turned the job over to his wife) the Doctor put him on guard inside the stall to see that the ani-mal was not molested by stupid visitors. The poor creature had a terrible time those first days. But when Jip told him how much money was being taken in, he determined to stick it out for John Dolittle's sake. And after a little while, although his opinion of the human race sank very low, he got sort of used to the silly, gaping faces of his audiences and gazed back at them—from both his heads—with fear-less superiority and the scorn that they deserved.

"Too-Too was always there"

Poor Dab-Dab was busier than ever now. For in addition
to the housekeeping duties she always had to keep one eye
on the Doctor; and many were the scoldings she gave him
because he would let the children in for nothing when she
wasn't looking.

At the end of each day Blossom, the manager, came to
divide up the money. And Too-Too, the mathematician, was
always there when the adding was done, to see that the Doctor got his proper share.

Although the pushmi-pullyu was so popular, the Doctor
saw very early in his new career that it would take quite a

time to earn sufficient money to pay the sailor back for the boat—let alone to make enough for himself and his family to live on besides.

He was rather sorry about this, for there were a lot of things in the circus business that he did not like and he was anxious to leave it. While his own show was a perfectly honest affair, there were many features of the circus that were faked; and the Doctor, who always hated fake of any kind, had an uncomfortable feeling that he was part of an establishment not strictly honest. Most of the gambling games were arranged so that those who played them were bound to lose their money.

But the thing that worried the Doctor most was the condition of the animals. Their life, he felt, was in most cases an unhappy one. At the end of his first day with the circus, after the crowds had gone home and all was quiet in the enclosure, he had gone back into the menagerie and talked to the animals there. They nearly all had complaints to make: their cages were not kept properly clean; they did not get exercise or room enough; with some, the food served was not the kind they liked.

The Doctor heard them all and was so indignant he sought out the ringmaster in his private caravan right away and told him plainly all the things he thought ought to be changed.

Blossom listened patiently until he had finished and then he laughed.

"Why, Doc," said he, "if I was to do all the things you want me to, I might as well leave the business! I'd be ruined. What, pension off the horses? Send the hurri-gurri back to his home? Keep the men cleaning out the cages all day? Buy special foods? Have the animals took out for walks every day, like a young ladies' academy? Man, you must be crazy! Now, look here: You don't know anything about this game—

nothing, see? I've given in to you in all you asked. I'm letting you run your part of the show your own way. But I'm going to run the rest of it my way. Understand? I don't want no interference. It's bad enough to have the strong man on the sick list. I ain't going to go broke just to please your Sunday school ideas. And that's flat."

Sad at heart, the Doctor left the manager's quarters and made his way across to his own caravan. On the steps of his wagon, he found the cat's-meat man smoking his evening pipe. Close by, Beppo, the old horse, was cropping the scrubby grass of the enclosure by the light of the moon.

"Nice night," said Matthew. "You look kind of worried, Doctor. Anything wrong?"

"Yes," said John Dolittle, sitting down miserably on the steps beside him. "Everything's wrong. I've just been talking to Blossom about improving conditions in the menagerie. He won't do a single thing I ask. I think I'll leave the circus."

"Oh, come now," said Matthew. "Why, you ain't hardly begun, Doctor! Blossom doesn't know yet that you can talk animal language even! Circuses don't have to be bad. *You* could run one that would be a new kind. Clean, honest, special—one that everybody in the world would come to see. But you got to get money first. Don't give up so easy."

"No, it's no use, Matthew. I'm doing no good here and I can't stay and see animals unhappy. I never should have gone into the business."

At this moment the old horse, Beppo, hearing his friend's voice, drew near and pushed his muzzle affectionately into the Doctor's ear.

"Hulloa," said John Dolittle. "Beppo, I'm afraid I can be of no help to you. I'm sorry—but I am going to leave the circus."

"But, Doctor," said the old horse, "you're our one hope.

Why, only today I heard the elephant and the talking horse —the cob who performs in the big show—they were saying how glad they were that you had come. Be patient. You can't change everything in a minute. If you go, then we'll never get anything we want. But we know that if you stay, before long you will be running the whole show the way it should be run. We're not worried as long as you're with us. Only stay. And mark my words, the day will come when the new circus, 'the Dolittle Circus,' will be the greatest on earth."

For a moment the Doctor was silent. And Matthew, who had not understood the conversation with the horse, waited impatiently for him to speak.

At last he arose and turned to go into the caravan.

"Well," said the cat's-meat man anxiously, "are you going to stay?"

"Yes, Matthew," said the Doctor. "It seems I've got to. Good night."

At the end of that week the Grimbledon Fair was over and the circus had to move on to the next town. It was a big job, this packing up a large show for a long journey by road. And all day Sunday the enclosure was a very busy place. Men ran around everywhere shouting orders. The big tent and the little tents were pulled down and rolled up. The stands were taken apart and piled into wagons. The large space that had looked so gay was quickly changed into a drab, untidy mess. It was all very new to the Doctor's pets; and though Dab-Dab joined in the general hustle of packing, the rest of them enjoyed the excitement and the newness of it no end.

Then in a long procession of caravans the circus set out upon the road. The next town to be visited was fifty miles off. This journey could not, of course, be covered in a single day, going at a walk. The nights were to be spent camping

"On the scent of a fox"

out by the roadside or in whatever convenient clear spaces could be found.

This part of the life, the halting for sleep, seemed to be enjoyed by all. When the kettle was put on to boil over the roadside fire everyone cheered up and got talkative. Jip's two friends, the clown's dog, Swizzle, and Toby, the Punch-and-Judy dog, always came around as soon as the procession stopped for the night and joined the Doctor's party. They, too, seemed to be much in favor of John Dolittle's taking charge of the show or running a circus of his own. And when they weren't amusing the family circle with wonderful stories of a show-dog's life they kept telling the Doctor that a real Dolittle Circus would, to their way of thinking, be a perfect institution.

John Dolittle had always said that there were just as many different characters and types among dogs as there were among people—in fact, more. He had written a book to prove this. He called it *Dog Psychology*. Most metaphysicians had pooh-poohed it, saying that no one but a hairbrain would write on such a subject. But this was only to hide the fact that they couldn't understand it.

Certainly these two, Swizzle, the clown's dog, and Toby, the Punch-and-Judy dog, had very different personalities. Swizzle (to look at, he was nothing but a common mongrel) had a great sense of humor. He made a joke out of everything. This may have been partly on account of his profession—helping a clown make people laugh. But it was also part of his philosophy. He told both the Doctor and Jip more than once that when he was still a puppy he had decided that nothing in this world was worth taking seriously. He was a great artist, nevertheless, and could always see the most difficult jokes—even when they were made at his own expense.

It was Swizzle's sense of humor that gave the Doctor the idea for the first comic papers printed for animals—when later he founded the Rat-and-Mouse Club. They were called *Cellar Life* and *Basement Humor* and were intended to bring light entertainment to those who live in dark places.

Toby, the other, was as different from his friend Swizzle as it is possible to be. He was a small dog, a dwarf white poodle. And he took himself and life quite seriously. The most noticeable thing about his character was his determination to get everything that he thought he ought to get. Yet he was not selfish, not at all. The Doctor always said that this shrewd businesslike quality was to be found in most little dogs—who had to make up for their small size by an extra share of cheek. The very first time Toby came visiting to John Dolittle's caravan he got on the Doctor's bed and made himself comfortable. Dab-Dab, highly scandalized, tried to put him off. But he wouldn't move. He said the Doctor didn't seem to mind and he was the owner of the bed. And from that time on he always occupied this place in the caravan's evening circle when he came to visit. He had won a special privilege for himself by sheer cheek. He was always demanding privileges, and he usually got them.

But there was one thing in which Toby and Swizzle were alike, and that was the pride they took in their personal friendship with John Dolittle, whom they considered the greatest man on earth.

One night on the first trip between towns the procession had stopped by the side of the road as usual. There was a nice old-fashioned farm quite near and Gub-Gub had gone off to see if there were any pigs in the sty. Otherwise the Doctor's family circle was complete. And soon after the kettle had been put on to boil, along came Toby and Swizzle. The night was cool; so instead of making a fire outside, Dab-Dab was using the stove in the caravan, and everybody was sitting around it chatting.

"Have you heard the news, Doctor?" said Toby, jumping up on the bed.

"No," said John Dolittle. "What is it?"

"At the next town—Ashby, you know, quite a large place—we are to pick up Sophie."

"Who in the world is Sophie?" asked the Doctor, getting out his slippers from behind the stove.

"She left us before you joined," said Swizzle. "Sophie's the performing seal—balances balls on her nose and does tricks

"Toby and Swizzle"

in the water. She fell sick and Blossom had to leave her
behind about a month ago. She's all right now, though, and
her keeper is meeting us at Ashby so she can join us again.
She's rather a sentimental sort of girl, is Sophie. But she's a
good sport, and I'm sure you will like her."

The circus reached Ashby about nine o'clock on a
Wednesday evening. It was to open to the public the first
thing the following morning. So all through that night, by
the light of flares, the men were busy hoisting tents, setting
up booths, and spreading tanbark. Even after the pushmi-
pullyu's stand was put together and the Doctor's family re-

"Climbed wearily from his bed"

tired to rest, no one got any sleep, for the ground still shook with the hammers driving pegs and the air was full of shouts and the spirit of work, till the dusk of dawn crept over the roofs of Ashby and showed the city of canvas that had been built in a night.

John Dolittle decided, as he climbed wearily from his bed, that circus life took a lot of getting used to. After breakfast, leaving Matthew in charge of his stand, he set out to make the acquaintance of the performing seal.

· The Sixth Chapter ·

SOPHIE, FROM ALASKA

SOPHIE'S keeper, like the rest of the showmen, had by this time got his part of the circus in readiness to open to the public. The seal was accustomed to perform in the big tent twice a day, following the Pinto brothers (trapeze acrobats) and the talking horse. But during the rest of the day she was a sideshow like the pushmi-pullyu. Here in an enclosed tank she dived after fish for the amusement of anyone who paid threepence to come and see her.

This morning—it was still quite early—Sophie's keeper was eating his breakfast outside on the steps when the Doctor entered the stand. Inside, a tank about twelve feet across had been let into the ground, and around it was a platform with a railing where visitors stood to watch the performance. Sophie, a fine five-foot Alaskan seal, with sleek skin and intelligent eyes, was wallowing moodily in the water of the tank. When the Doctor spoke to her in her own language, and she realized who her visitor was, she burst into a flood of tears.

"What is the matter?" asked John Dolittle.

The seal, still weeping, did not answer.

"Calm yourself," said the Doctor. "Don't be hysterical. Tell me, are you still sick? I understood you had recovered."

"Oh, yes, I got over that," said Sophie through her tears. "It was only an upset stomach. They *will* feed us this stale fish, you know."

"Then what's the matter?" asked the Doctor. "Why are you crying?"

"I was weeping for joy," said Sophie. "I was just thinking as you came in that the only person in the world who could help me in my trouble was John Dolittle. Of course, I had heard all about you through the post office and the *Arctic Monthly*. In fact, I had written to you. It was I who contributed those articles on underwater swimming. You remember? The Alaskan Wiggle—you know—double overhand stroke. It was printed in the August number of your magazine. We were awfully sorry when you had to give up the *Arctic Monthly*. It was tremendously popular among the seals."

"But what was this trouble you were speaking of?" asked the Doctor.

"Oh, yes," said Sophie, bursting into tears again. "That just shows you how glad I am; I had forgotten all about it for the moment. You know, when you first came in I thought you were an ordinary visitor. But the very first word of sealish that you spoke—and Alaskan sealish at that—I knew who you were: John Dolittle, the one man in the world I wanted to see! It was too much, I—"

"Come, come!" said the Doctor. "Don't break down again. Tell me what your trouble is."

"Well," said Sophie, "it's this: While I—"

At that moment there was a noise outside, the rattling of a bucket.

"Sh! It's the keeper coming," whispered the Doctor

quickly. "Just carry on with your tricks. I'm not letting them know I can talk to the animals."

When the keeper entered to swab the floor, Sophie was frisking and diving for an audience of one: a quiet little fat man with a battered high hat on the back of his head. The keeper just glanced at him, before setting to work, and decided that he was quite an ordinary person, nobody in particular at all.

As soon as the man had finished his mopping and disappeared again, Sophie continued:

"You know," said the seal, "when I fell sick we were performing at Hatley-on-Sea, and I and my keeper—Higgins is his name—stayed there two weeks while the circus went on without us. Now, there's a zoo at Hatley—only a small one—near the esplanade. They have artificial ponds there with seals and otters in them. Well, Higgins got talking to the keeper of these seals one day and told him about my being sick. And they decided I needed company. So they put me in the pond with the other seals till I should recover. Among them there was an older one who came from the same part of the Bering Straits as I did. He gave me some very bad news about my husband. It seems that ever since I was captured he has been unhappy and refused to eat. He used to be leader of the herd. But after I was taken away he had worried and grown thin and finally another seal was elected leader in his place. Now he wasn't expected to live." Quietly Sophie began to weep again. "I can quite understand it. We were devoted to one another. And although he was so big and strong and no other seal in the herd ever dared to argue with him, without me, well, he was just lost, you know—a mere baby. He relied on me for everything. And now—I don't know what's happening to him. It's just terrible—terrible!"

" 'I ought to go to him' "

"Well, wait a minute," said the Doctor. "Don't cry. What do you think ought to be done?"

"I ought to go to him," said Sophie, raising herself in the water and spreading out her flippers. "I ought to be by his side. He is the proper leader of the herd and he needs me. I hoped I might escape at Hatley, but not a chance did I get."

"Humph!" muttered the Doctor. "It's an awful long way to the Bering Straits. How on earth would you get there?"

"That's just what I wanted to see you about," said Sophie. "Overland, of course, my rate of travel is very slow. If I could only have gotten away at Hatley I'd have been all

right. Because, of course," she added with a powerful swish
of her tail that slopped half the water out of the tank, "once
I reached the sea I'd be up to Alaska in no time."

"Ah, yes," the Doctor agreed, as he shook the water out of
his boots. "I see you are a powerful swimmer. How far are
we from the coast here?"

"About a hundred miles," said Sophie. "Oh, dear! Poor
Slushy! My poor, poor Slushy!"

"Poor who?" asked the Doctor.

"Slushy," said the seal. "That's my husband's name. He
relied on me in everything, poor, simple Slushy. What shall
I do? What *shall* I do?"

"Well, now listen," said John Dolittle. "This is no easy matter, to smuggle you to the sea. I don't say it's impossible. But
it needs thinking out. Perhaps I can get you free some other
way—openly. In the meantime I'll send word up to your
husband by bird messenger and tell him to stop worrying
because you are all right. And the same messenger can
bring us back news of how he is getting on. Now, cheer up.
Here come some people to see you perform."

A schoolmistress with a band of children entered, accompanied by Higgins, the keeper. As they came in a little fat
man went out, smiling to himself. Soon the children were
laughing with delight at the antics of the big animal in the
tank. And Higgins decided that Sophie must now be feeling
entirely recovered, for he had never seen her so sprightly or
so full of good spirits before.

· The Seventh Chapter ·

THE MESSENGER FROM THE NORTH

LATE that night the Doctor took Too-Too with him and went to visit the seal again. "Now, Sophie," said he when they had reached the side of the tank, "this owl is a friend of mine, and I want you to describe to him just where in Alaska your husband can be found. Then we'll send him off to the seashore, and he will hand on your message to the gulls who are going northwestward. Let me introduce you: Sophie, this is Too-Too, one of the cleverest birds I know. He is particularly good at mathematics."

The owl sat on the rail while Sophie told him exactly how Slushy could be reached and reeled off a long and loving message for her husband. When she had ended he said, "I think I'll make for Bristol, Doctor. It is about the nearest coast town. There are always plenty of gulls to be found in the harbor. I'll get one to take this and pass it on to its destination."

"Very good, Too-Too," said the Doctor. "But we want to hurry it all we can. If you can find some seabird who is willing to take it the whole way as a special favor to me, it would be better."

"All right," said Too-Too, preparing to depart. "Leave the window of the caravan open, so I can get in. I don't suppose I shall be back much before two in the morning. So long!"

Then the Doctor returned to his wagon and rewrote the last part of his new book, which was called *Animal Natation.* Sophie had given him a lot of helpful hints on good swimming style, which made it necessary for him to add three more chapters.

He got so interested in this he did not notice how the time was passing till, somewhere between two and three in the morning, he suddenly found Too-Too, the night bird, standing on the table before him.

"Doctor," said he, speaking low so he would not wake the animals. "You could never guess whom I met. You remember the gull who brought you the warning about Cape Stephen Light? Well, I ran into him in Bristol harbor. I hadn't seen him since the good old houseboat days. But I recognized him at once. I told him I was hunting for someone to take a message up to Alaska; and when he heard it was you who sent me, he said he would attend to it himself with pleasure. He doesn't expect to be back under five days, though—at best."

"Splendid, Too-Too, splendid!" said the Doctor.

"I am returning to Bristol Friday," said the owl, "and if he isn't back then, I'll wait till he comes."

The following morning John Dolittle told Sophie that her message had been sent on, and she was very pleased. For the present there was nothing further to be done but to wait for the gull's return.

On Thursday (a day before the time Too-Too had planned to return to Bristol) the Doctor's whole party was seated around the table in the caravan listening to a story from Toby, the Punch-and-Judy dog. Just as Toby paused breathless at the most exciting part, there came a gentle tapping on the window.

"Booh!" said Gub-Gub. "How spookish!" And he crawled under the bed.

John Dolittle rose, drew back the curtains, and opened the window. On the sill stood the gull who months before had brought him another message by night when he lived in the houseboat post office. Now, weather-beaten and weary, he looked more dead than alive. Gently the Doctor lifted him from the windowsill, and set him down on the table. Then they all drew near, staring at him in silence, waiting for the exhausted bird to speak.

"John Dolittle," said the gull at last, "I didn't wait for Too-Too to meet me in Bristol because I thought you ought to know at once. The seal herd to which Sophie and her husband belonged is in a bad way—very bad. And it has all come about because Sophie was taken away and her husband, Slushy, lost the leadership. Winter has set in up there early this year—and my, such a winter! Blizzards, mountainous snowdrifts, the seas frozen months ahead of the usual time. I nearly died of the cold myself—and you know we gulls can stand awful low temperatures. Well, leadership for the seal herds is tremendously important in bad weather. They're not much different from sheep—same as all animals that travel and live in packs. And without a big, strong boss to lead them to the open fishing and the protected wintering places, they're just lost, that's all—helpless. Now, it seems, ever since Slushy started to mope they've had one leader after another—and none of them any good. Rows and little revolutions going on in the herd all the while. And in the meantime the walruses and sea lions are driving them out of all the best fishing and the Eskimo seal hunters killing them right and left. No seal herd can last long against the fur hunters up there if they haven't got a

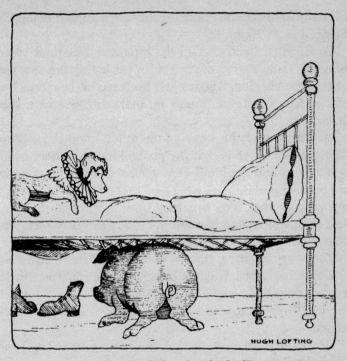

"He crawled under the bed"

good leader with wits enough to keep them out of danger. Slushy was the best they ever had, as strong as an ox. Now all he does is lie on an iceberg, mooning and weeping because his favorite wife's been taken away. He's got hundreds more, just as good-looking, but the only one he wants is Sophie, and there you are. The herd's just going to pieces. In the days of Slushy's leadership, they tell me, it was the finest seal herd in the Arctic Circle. Now, most likely, with this extra bad winter setting in, it'll be wiped right out."

For fully a minute after the gull finished his long speech silence reigned in the caravan.

Finally John Dolittle said, "Toby, does Sophie belong to Blossom or to Higgins?"

"To Higgins, Doctor," said the little dog. "He does something the same as you do; in return for letting the seal perform in the big ring, Higgins gets his stand in the circus free and pockets whatever money he makes on her as a sideshow."

"Well, that *isn't* the same as me at all," said the Doctor. "The big difference is that the pushmi-pullyu is here of his own accord and Sophie is kept against her will. It is a perfect scandal that hunters can go up to the Arctic and capture any animals they like, breaking up families and upsetting herd government and community life in this way—a crying shame! Toby, how much does a seal cost?"

"They vary in price, Doctor," said Toby. "But I heard Sophie say that when Higgins bought her in Liverpool from the men who had caught her he paid twenty pounds for her. She had been trained on the ship to do tricks before she landed."

"How much have we got in the money box, Too-Too?" asked the Doctor.

"All of last week's gate money," said the owl, "except one shilling and threepence. The threepence you spent to get your hair cut and the shilling went on celery for Gub-Gub."

"Well, what does that bring the total to?"

Too-Too, the mathematician, cocked his head on one side and closed his left eye—as he always did when calculating.

"Two pounds, seven shillings," he murmured, "minus one shilling and threepence leaves—er—leaves—two pounds, five shillings, and ninepence, cash in hand, net."

"Good Lord!" groaned the Doctor, "barely enough to buy a tenth of Sophie! I wonder if there's anyone I could borrow from. That's the only good thing about being a people's doctor. When I had a practice I could borrow from my patients."

"If I remember rightly," muttered Dab-Dab, "it was more often your patients that borrowed from you."

"Blossom wouldn't let you buy her even if you had the money," said Swizzle. "Higgins is under contract—made a promise—to travel with the circus for a year."

"Very well, then," said the Doctor. "There's only one thing to be done. That seal doesn't belong to those men, anyhow. She's a free citizen of the Arctic Circle. And if she wants to go back there, back she shall go. Sophie must escape."

Before his pets went to bed that night the Doctor made them promise that for the present they would say nothing to the seal about the bad news the gull had brought. It would only worry her, he told them. And until he had helped her to get safely to the sea there was no need for her to know.

Then, until the early hours of the morning, he sat up with Matthew making plans for Sophie's flight. At first the cat's-meat man was very much against the idea.

"Why, Doctor," said he, "you'll get arrested if you're caught. Helping that seal escape from her owner! They'll call it stealing."

"I don't care that much," said the Doctor snapping his fingers. "Let them call it what they like. Let them arrest me—if they catch me. If the case is taken to the courts, at least I'll get a chance to say a word for the rights of wild animals."

"They won't listen to you, Doctor," said Matthew. "They'll say you're a sentimental crank. Higgins would win easy. Rights of property and all that. I see your point, but the judge wouldn't. He'd tell you to pay Higgins his twenty pounds for a lost seal. And if you couldn't, you'd go to jail."

"I don't care," the Doctor repeated. "But listen, Matthew: I

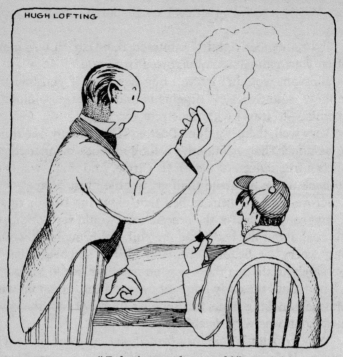

HUGH LOFTING

" 'I don't care that much' "

wouldn't want you to get mixed up in it if you don't think
it's right. I shall have to use deception if I'm to be successful.
And I should be very sorry to get you into trouble. If you
would prefer to stay clear of it, say so now. But for my part,
my mind is made up: Sophie is going to Alaska even if I
have to go to jail—that will be nothing new. I've been in jail
before."

"So have I," said the cat's-meat man. "Was you ever in
Cardiff Jail? By Jingo! that's a rotten one! The worst I was
ever in."

"No," said the Doctor. "I've only been in African jails—as

yet. They're bad enough. But let us get back to the point. Would you sooner not help me in this? It's against the law— I know—even if I think the law is wrong. Understand, I shan't be the least offended if you have conscientious objections to aiding and abetting me. Eh?"

"Conscientious objections, me eye!" said the cat's-meat man, opening the window and spitting accurately out into the night. "O' course, I'll help you, Doctor. That old sour-faced Higgins ain't got no right to that seal. She's a free creature of the seas. If he paid twenty pounds for her, more fool him. What you say goes, Doctor. Ain't we kind of partners in this here circus business? I think it's a good kind of a lark meself. Didn't I tell you I was venturesome? Lor' bless us! I done worse things than help a performin' seal to elope. Why, that time I was telling you of, when I was jailed in Cardiff—do you know what it was for?"

"No, I have no idea," said the Doctor. "Some slight error, I have no doubt. Now let us—"

"It was no slight error," said Matthew, "I—"

"Well, never mind it now," said John Dolittle quickly. "We all make mistakes, you know." ("It was no mistake, neither," muttered Matthew as the Doctor hurried on.) "If you are quite sure that you will have no regrets about going into this —er—matter with me, let us consider ways and means. It will be necessary, I think, in order to avoid getting Blossom suspicious, for me to leave the circus for a few days. I will say I have business to attend to—which is quite true, even if I don't attend to it. But it would look very queer if I and Sophie disappeared the same night. So I will go first, leaving you in charge of my show. Then a day—or better, two days —later, Sophie will disappear."

"Also on business," put in Matthew, chuckling. "You mean

you'll leave me the job of letting her out of her tank after you're gone?"

"Yes, if you don't mind," said the Doctor.

"It'll give me great pleasure," said the cat's-meat man.

"Splendid!" said the Doctor. "I'll arrange beforehand with Sophie where she is to meet me, once she's clear of the circus. And then—"

"And then your job will begin in earnest," Matthew Mugg said with a laugh.

PART II

· The First Chapter ·

PLANNING THE ESCAPE

ALTHOUGH the plans for Sophie's escape were of course kept a strict secret from any of the people in Blossom's establishment, the animals of the circus soon got to know of them through Jip, Toby, and Swizzle. And for days before the flight took place it was the one subject of conversation in the menagerie, in the stables, and in the Doctor's caravan.

When John Dolittle returned from telling Blossom that he was about to leave the circus on business for a few days, he found his own animals seated about the table in the wagon talking in whispers.

"Well, Doctor," said Matthew, who was sitting on the steps, "did you speak to the boss?"

"Yes," said the Doctor. "I told him. It's all right. I'm leaving tonight. I felt frightfully guilty, and underhanded. I do wish I could do this openly."

"You'd stand a fat chance of succeeding, if you did!" said Matthew. "I don't feel guilty none."

"Listen, Doctor," said Jip. "All the circus animals are tremendously interested in your scheme. They've asked if

59

there's anything they can do to help. When is Sophie going to get away?"

"The day after tomorrow," said John Dolittle. "Matthew, here, will undo the door of her stand just after closing time. But listen, Matthew: You'll have to be awfully careful no one sees you tinkering with the lock. If we *should* get caught we would indeed be in a bad fix then. Tinkering with locks makes it a felony instead of a misdemeanor, or something like that. Do be careful, won't you?"

"You can rely on me, Doctor," said the cat's-meat man, proudly puffing out his chest. "I've got a way of me own with locks, I have. No force, sort of persuasion like."

"Get clear out of the way as soon as you have let her free," said the Doctor, "so you won't be connected with it at all. Dear me, how like a low-down conspiracy it sounds!"

"Sounds like lots of fun to me," said Matthew.

"To me, too," said Jip.

"It'll be the best trick that's been done in this show for a long while," put in Swizzle. "Ladies and gentleman: John Dolittle, the world-famous conjurer, will now make a live seal disappear from the stage before your eyes. Abracadabra, mumble-and-jabberer, hoopla, hey presto! *Gone!*"

And Swizzle stood on his hind legs and bowed to an imaginary audience behind the stove.

"Well," said the Doctor, "even though it sounds underhanded, I don't feel I'm doing anything wrong—myself. They've no right to keep Sophie in this slavery. How would you and I like it," he asked of Matthew, "to be made to dive for fish into a tub of dirty water for the amusement of loafers?"

"Rotten!" said Matthew. "I never did care for fish—nor water, neither. But look here, have you arranged with Sophie where she's to meet you?"

"Swizzle bowed to an imaginary audience"

"Yes," said John Dolittle. "As soon as she gets clear of the circus enclosure—and don't forget we are relying on you to leave the back gate open as well as Sophie's own door—as soon as she's out of the fence, she is to cross the road where she will find an empty house. Alongside of that there is a little dark passage, and in that passage I will be waiting for her. My goodness, I do hope everything goes right! It's so dreadfully important for her—and for all those seals in Alaska, too."

"And what are you going to do then," asked Matthew, "when she's got as far as the passage?"

"Well, it's no use trying to plan too far as to detail. My general idea is to make for the Bristol Channel. That's about our shortest cut to the sea from here. Once there, she's all right. But it's nearly a hundred miles as the crow flies; and as we'll have to keep concealed most of the way I'm not expecting an easy journey. However, there's no sense in meeting your troubles halfway. I've no doubt we shall get along all right once she's safely away from the circus."

Many of the Doctor's pets wanted to accompany him on his coming adventure. Jip tried especially hard to be taken. But in spite of his great desire to have the assistance of his friends, John Dolittle felt that he would arouse less suspicion if he left his entire family with the circus just as it was.

So that night after a final talk with Sophie he set out alone —on business. He took with him most of what money he had, leaving a little with Matthew to pay for the small needs of his establishment while he was away. His "business," as a matter of fact, did not take him further than the next town —which journey he made by a stagecoach. In those days, you see, although there were railroads, to be sure, they were as yet very scarce. And most of the cross-country traveling between the smaller towns was still done in the old-fashioned way.

On his arrival at the next town he took a room in an inn and remained there the whole time. Two nights later he returned to Ashby after dark and, entering the town from the far side, made his way through unfrequented streets till he reached the passage that was to be his meeting place with Sophie.

Now all his pets, though they had not been given any particular parts to play in the plot of Sophie's escape, were determined to do anything they could to help things on their own account—which, as you will see, turned out to be a good deal. And as they waited for the arrival of the ap-

"Made his way through unfrequented streets"

pointed hour their excitement (which Gub-Gub, for one, had hard work to conceal) grew every minute.

About ten o'clock, when the circus was beginning to close up, Too-Too stationed himself on top of the menagerie where he could see everything that went on. He had arranged with the elephant and the animals of the collection to start a rumpus in the menagerie on a given signal—to attract, if necessary, the attention of the circus men away from the escaping seal. Gub-Gub gave himself the job of watching Blossom, and he took up a post underneath the ringmaster's private caravan.

There was a full moon, and even after the circus lamps were put out there was still a good deal of light. The Doctor would have postponed the escape on this account until later, but he realized that the state of affairs among the Alaskan seals made it necessary for Sophie to get away as soon as possible.

Well, about an hour after Blossom had locked up the fence gates and retired to his caravan, Matthew slipped away from the pushmi-pullyu's stand and sauntered off across the enclosure. Jip, also pretending he was doing nothing in particular, followed him at a short distance. Everyone seemed to be abed and not a soul did Matthew meet till he came to the gate the Doctor had spoken of. Making sure that no one saw him, the cat's-meat man quickly undid the latch and set the gate ajar. Then he strolled away toward Sophie's stand while Jip remained to watch the gate.

He hadn't been gone more than a minute when along came the circus watchman with a lantern. He closed the gate and, to Jip's horror, locked it with a key. Jip, still pretending he was just sniffing around the fence after rats, waited till the man had disappeared again. Then he raced off toward Sophie's stand to find Matthew.

Now things had not turned out for the cat's-meat man as easy as he had expected. On approaching the seal's tank house, he had seen from a distance the figure of Higgins sitting on the steps smoking and looking at the moon. Matthew therefore withdrew into the shadow of a tent and waited till the seal's keeper should go away to bed.

Higgins, he knew, slept in a wagon close to Blossom's on the other side of the enclosure. But while he watched and waited, instead of Higgins going away, another figure, the watchman's, came, joined the man on the steps, sat down, and started chatting. Presently Jip, smelling out Matthew behind the tent, came up and tried frantically to make him understand that the gate he had opened had been closed again and locked.

Jip had very little success in trying to make the cat's-meat man understand him, and for nearly an hour Matthew stayed in the shadow waiting for the two figures on the steps of Sophie's stand to move away and leave the coast clear for him to let the seal free. In the meantime John Dolittle in his narrow, dark passage outside the circus enclosure wondered what the delay was and tried to read his watch by the dim light of the moon.

Finally Matthew decided that the two men were never going to bed. So, swearing under his breath, he crept away from the shadow of the tent and set off to seek Theodosia, his wife.

On arrival at his own wagon he found her darning socks by the light of the candle.

"*Pst!* Theodosia," he whispered through the window. "Listen."

"Good Lord!" gasped Mrs. Mugg, dropping her needlework. "What a fright you gave me, Matthew! Is it all right? Has the seal got away?"

"No, it's all wrong. Higgins and the watchman are sitting on the steps talking. I can't get near the door while they're there. Go up and draw 'em off for me, will yer? Tell 'em a tent's blown down or something—anything to get 'em away. They're going to set there all night if something ain't done."

"All right," said Theodosia. "Wait till I get my shawl. I'll bring them over here for some cocoa."

Then the helpful Mrs. Mugg went off and invited Higgins and the watchman to come to her husband's wagon for a little party. Matthew would be along to join them presently, she said.

"His nimble fingers soon had the door unlocked"

As soon as the coast was clear the cat's-meat man sped up the steps of the seal's stand and, in a minute, his nimble fingers had the door unlocked. Just inside lay Sophie, all ready to start out upon her long journey. With a grunt of thanks she waddled forth into the moonlight, slid down the steps, and set off clumsily toward the gate.

Once more Jip tried his hardest to make Matthew understand that something was wrong. But the cat's-meat man merely took the dog's signals of distress for joy and marched off to join his wife's cocoa party, feeling that his share of the night's work had been well done.

In the meantime Sophie had waddled her way laboriously to the gate and found it locked.

Jip had then gone all around the fence, trying to find a hole big enough for her to get through. But he met with no success. Poor Sophie had escaped the captivity of her tank only to find herself still a prisoner within the circus enclosure.

Everything that had happened up to this had been carefully watched by a little round bird perched on the roof of the menagerie. Too-Too, the listener, the night seer, the mathematician, was more than usually wide-awake. And presently, while Jip was still nosing around the fence, trying to find Sophie a way out, he heard the whir of wings over his head and an owl alighted by his side.

"For heaven's sake, Jip," whispered Too-Too, "keep your head. The game will be up if you don't. You're doing no good by running around like that. Get Sophie into hiding—push her under the flap of a tent or something. Look at her, laying out in the moonlight there, as though this were Greenland! If anyone should come along and see her we're lost. Hide her until Matthew sees what has happened to the gate. Hurry—I see someone coming."

As Too-Too flew back to his place on the menagerie roof, Jip rushed off to Sophie and in a few hurried words explained the situation to her.

"Come over here," he said. "Get under the skirt of this tent. So! Gosh! Only just in time! There's the light of a lantern moving. Now lie perfectly still and wait till I come and tell you."

And in his little dark passage beyond the circus fence John Dolittle once more looked at his watch and muttered, "What *can* have happened? Will she never come?"

It was not many minutes after Matthew had joined the

cocoa party in his own wagon that the watchman rose from the table and said he ought to be getting along on his rounds. The cat's-meat man, anxious to give Sophie as much time as possible to get away, tried to persuade him to stay.

"Oh, stop and have another cup of cocoa!" said he. "This is a quiet town. Nobody's going to break in. Fill your pipe and let's chat awhile."

"No," said the watchman, "thank ye. I'd like to, but I mustn't. Blossom give me strict orders to keep movin' the whole night. If he was to come and not find me on the job, I'd catch it hot."

And in spite of everything Matthew could do to keep him, the watchman took his lamp and left.

Higgins, however, remained. And while the cat's-meat man and his wife talked pleasantly to him of politics and the weather, they expected any moment to hear a shout outside warning the circus that Sophie had escaped.

But the watchman, when he found the stand open and empty, did not begin by shouting. He came running back to Matthew's wagon.

"Higgins," he yelled, "your seal's gone!"

"Gone!" cried Higgins. *"Gone!"* said Matthew. "Can't be possible!"

"I tell you she 'as," said the watchman. " 'Er door's open and she ain't there."

"Good heavens!" cried Higgins, springing up. "I could swear I locked the door as usual. But if the gates in the fence was all closed, she can't be far away. We can soon find 'er again. Come on!"

And he ran out of the wagon—with Matthew and Theodosia, pretending to be greatly disturbed, close at his heels.

"I'll go take another look at the gates," said the watchman.

"I'm sure they're all right. But I'll make double certain anyway."

Then Higgins, Matthew, and Theodosia raced off for the seal's stand.

"The door's open, sure enough," said Matthew as they came up to it. " 'Ow very peculiar!"

"Let's go inside," said Higgins. "Maybe she's hiding at the bottom of the tank."

Then all three of them went in and by the light of matches peered down into the dark water.

Meanwhile the watchman turned up again.

"The gates are all right," he said, "—closed and locked, every one of them."

Then at last Matthew knew something had gone wrong. And while Higgins and the watchman were examining the water with the lamp, he whispered something to his wife, slipped out, and ran for the gate, hoping Theodosia would keep the other two at the stand long enough for his purpose.

As a matter of fact she played her part very well, did Mrs. Mugg. Presently Higgins said, "There ain't nothing under the water. Sophie's not here. Let's go outside and look for her."

Then just as the two men turned to leave, Theodosia cried, "What's that?"

"What's what?" said Higgins, turning back.

"That—down there," said Mrs. Mugg, pointing into the dirty water. "I thought I saw something move. Bring the lantern nearer."

The watchman crouched over the edge of the tank; and Higgins, beside him, screwed up his eyes to see better.

"I don't see nothing," said the keeper.

"Oh! Oh! I'm feeling faint!" cried Mrs. Mugg. "Help me. I'm going to fall in!"

" 'Oh! Oh! I'm feeling faint!' "

And Theodosia, a heavy woman, swayed and suddenly crumpled up on top of the two crouching men.

Then, *splash! splash!* in fell, not Theodosia, but Higgins and the watchman—lamp and all.

· The Second Chapter ·

"ANIMALS' NIGHT" AT THE CIRCUS

THE white mouse was the only one of the Doctor's pets that witnessed that scene in Sophie's tank house when Mrs. Mugg pushed the two men into the water by-accident-on-purpose. And for weeks afterward he used to entertain the Dolittle family circle with his description of Mr. Higgins, the seal keeper, diving for fish and coming up for air.

That was one of the busiest and jolliest nights the circus ever had—from the animals' point of view; and the two men falling in the water and yelling for help was the beginning of a grand and noble racket, which lasted for a good half hour and finally woke every soul in Ashby out of his sleep.

First of all, Blossom, hearing cries of alarm, came rushing out of his caravan. At the foot of the steps a pig appeared from nowhere, rushed between his legs, and brought him down on his nose. Throughout the whole proceedings Gub-Gub never let Blossom get very far without popping out from behind something and upsetting him.

Next Fatima, the snake charmer, ran from her boudoir with a candle in one hand and a hammer in the other. She hadn't gone two steps before a mysterious duck flew over

71

"A small pig tripped him up"

her head and, with one sweep of its wing, blew the candle out. Fatima ran back, relit the candle, and tried again to go to the rescue. But the same thing happened. Dab-Dab kept Fatima almost as busy as Gub-Gub kept Blossom.

Then Mrs. Blossom, hastily donning a dressing gown, appeared upon the scene. She was met by the old horse Beppo, who had a habit of asking people for sugar. She tried to get by him and Beppo moved out of her way. But in doing so he trod on her corns so badly that she went howling back to bed again and did not reappear.

But although the animals managed by various tricks to

keep many people occupied, they could not attend to all the circus folk; and before long the watchman and Higgins, yelling murder in the tank, had attracted a whole lot of tent riggers and other showmen to Sophie's stand.

Now, in the meantime, Matthew Mugg had reopened the gate in the fence. But when he looked around for Sophie she was nowhere to be seen. Jip and Too-Too, as a matter of fact, were the only ones who really knew where she was. Jip, however, with all this crowd of men rushing around the seal's stand near the gate, was afraid to give Sophie the word to leave her hiding place. More of Blossom's men kept arriving and adding to the throng. Several lanterns were lit and brought onto the scene. Everybody was shouting, one half asking what the matter was, the other half telling them. Mr. Blossom, after being thrown down in the mud by Gub-Gub for the sixth time, was hitting everyone he met and bellowing like a mad bull. The hubbub and confusion were awful.

At last Higgins and the watchman were fished out of their bathtub and, highly perfumed with kerosene and fish, they joined the hunt.

The watchman and everyone were sure that Sophie must be somewhere near—which was quite true: the tent, under the skirt of which she was lying, was only thirty feet from her stand. But the gate by which she was to pass out was also quite near.

While Jip was wondering when the men would move away so he could let her go, Higgins cried out that he had found a track in the soft earth. Then a dozen lanterns were brought forward, and the men started to follow the trail that Sophie had left behind on the way to her hiding place.

Luckily, with so many feet crossing and recrossing the same part of the enclosure, the flipper marks were not easy to make out. Nevertheless, even with Matthew doing his best to lead them off on a wrong scent, the trackers steadily moved in the right direction—toward the tent where poor Sophie, the devoted wife, lay in hiding with a beating heart.

John Dolittle, waiting impatiently in his little passage, had heard the noise of shouting from the circus. He knew that meant that Sophie had gotten out from her stand. But as minute after minute went by and still she did not come to the meeting place, the Doctor's uneasiness increased a hundredfold.

But his anxiety was no worse than Jip's. Closer and closer the trackers came toward the spot where he had hidden the seal. The poor dog was in despair.

However, he had forgotten Too-Too the mathematician. From his lookout on the menagerie roof, away off on the far side of the enclosure, the little owl was still surveying the battlefield with a general's eye. He was waiting only till he was sure that all the circus folk had left their beds to join the hunt and that there were no more to come. When he played his masterstroke of strategy he did not want any extra interference from unexpected quarters.

Suddenly he flew down to a ventilator in the menagerie wall and hooted softly. Instantly there began within the most terrible pandemonium that was ever heard. The lion roared, the opossum shrieked, the yak bellowed, the hyena howled, the elephant trumpeted and stamped his floor into kindling wood. It was the grand climax to the animals' conspiracy.

On the other side of the enclosure the trackers and hunters stood still and listened.

"What in thunder's that?" asked Blossom.

"Coming from the menagerie, ain't it?" said one of the men. "Sounds like the elephant's broke loose."

"He stamped his floor into kindling wood"

"I know," said another: *"It's Sophie.* She's gotten into the menagerie and scared the elephant."

"That's it," said Blossom. "Lord, and us huntin' for 'er over here! To the menagerie!" And he grabbed up a lantern and started to run.

"To the menagerie!" yelled the crowd. And in a moment, to Jip's delight, they were all gone, rushing away to the other side of the enclosure.

All but one. Matthew Mugg, hanging back, pretending to do up his shoelace, saw Jip flash across to a small tent and disappear under the skirt.

"Now," said Jip. "Run, Sophie! Swim! Fly! Anything! Get out of the gate!"

Hopping and flopping, Sophie covered the ground as best she could, while Jip yelped to her to hurry and Matthew held the gate open. At last the seal waddled out onto the road, and the cat's-meat man saw her cross it and disappear into the passage alongside the deserted house. He closed the gate again and stamped out her tracks at the foot of it. Then he leaned against it, mopping his brow.

"Holy smoke!" he sighed. "And I told the Doctor I done worse things than help a seal escape! If I ever—"

A knock sounded on the gate at his back. With shaking hands he opened it once more; and there stood a policeman, his little bull's-eye lantern shining at his belt. Matthew's heart almost stopped beating. He had no love for policemen.

"I ain't done nothing!" he began. "I—"

"What's all the row about?" asked the constable. "You've got the whole town woke up. Lion broke loose or something?"

Matthew heaved a sigh of relief.

"No," he said. "Just a little trouble with the elephant. Got his leg caught in a rope and pulled a tent over. We 'ave 'im straightened out now. Nothing to worry about."

"Oh, is that all?" said the policeman. "Folks was going around asking if the end of the world was come. Good night!"

"Good night, constable!" Matthew closed the gate for the third time. "And give my love to all the little constables," he added under his breath as he set off for the menagerie.

And so at last John Dolittle, waiting, anxious and impatient, in the dark passage alongside the empty house, heard to his delight the sound of a peculiar footstep. A flipper-step, it should more properly be called; for the noise of Sophie traveling over a brick pavement was a curious mixture between someone slapping the ground with a wet rag and a sack of potatoes being yanked along a floor.

"Is that you, Sophie?" he whispered.

"Yes," said the seal, hitching herself forward to where the Doctor stood.

"Thank goodness! What in the world kept you so long?"

"Oh, there was some mix-up with the gates," said Sophie. "But hadn't we better be getting out of the town? It doesn't seem to me very safe here."

"There's no chance of that for the present," said the Doctor. "The noise they made in the circus has woken everybody. We dare not try and get through the streets now. I just saw a policeman pass across the end of the passage there—luckily for us, just after you popped into it."

"But then what are we going to do?"

"We'll have to stay here for the present. It would be madness to try and run for it now."

"Well, but suppose they come searching in here. We couldn't—"

At that moment two persons with lanterns stopped at the end of the passage, talked a moment, and moved away.

"Quite so," whispered the Doctor. "This isn't safe either. We must find a better place."

Now, on one side of this alleyway there was a high stone wall, and on the other a high brick wall. The brick wall enclosed the back garden belonging to the deserted house.

"If we could only get into that old empty house," murmured the Doctor. "We'd be safe to stay there as long as we wished—till this excitement among the townsfolk dies down. Can you think of any way you could get over that wall?"

The seal measured the height with her eye.

"Eight feet," she murmured. "I could do it with a ladder. I've been trained to walk up ladders. I do it in the circus, you know. Perhaps—"

"Sh!" whispered the Doctor. "There's the policeman's bull's-eye lantern again. Ah, thank goodness, he's passed on! Listen, there's just a chance I may find an orchard ladder in the garden. Now you wait here; lie flat and wait till I come back."

Then John Dolittle, a very active man in spite of his round figure, drew back and took a running jump at the wall. His fingers caught the top of it; he hauled himself up, threw one leg over, and dropped lightly down into a flower bed on the other side. At the bottom of the garden he saw in the moonlight what he guessed to be a toolshed. Slipping up to the door, he opened it and went in.

Inside his groping hands touched and rattled some empty flower pots. But he could find no ladder. He found a grass mower, a lawn roller, rakes and tools of every kind, but no ladder. And there seemed little hope of finding one in the dark. So he carefully closed the door, hung his coat over the dirty little cobwebby window, in order that no light should be seen from the outside, and struck a match.

And there, sure enough, hanging against the wall right above his head, was an orchard ladder just the right length. In a moment he had blown out the match, opened the door, and was marching down the garden with the ladder on his shoulder.

Standing it in a firm place, he scaled up and sat astride the wall. Next he pulled the ladder up after him, changed it across to the other side, and lowered the foot end into the passage.

Then John Dolittle, perched astride the top of the wall

(looking exactly like Humpty-Dumpty), whispered down into the dark passage below him, "Now climb up, Sophie. I'll keep this end steady. And when you reach the top get onto the wall beside me till I change the ladder over to the garden side. Don't get flustered now. Easy does it."

It was a good thing that Sophie was so well trained in balancing. Never in the circus had she performed a better trick than she did that night. It was a feat that even a person might well be proud of. But she knew that her freedom, the happiness of her husband, depended on her steadiness. And though she was in constant fear that any minute someone might come down the passage and discover them, it gave her a real thrill to turn the tables on her captors by using the skill they had taught her in the last grand performance to escape them.

Firmly, rung by rung, she began hoisting her heavy body upward. The ladder, fortunately, was longer than the height of the wall. Thus the Doctor had been able to set it at an easier, flattish slope instead of straight upright. With the seal's weight it sagged dangerously; and the Doctor on the wall prayed that it would prove strong enough. Being an orchard ladder for tree-pruning, it got very narrow at the top. And it was here, where there was hardly room enough for a seal's two front flappers to take hold, that the ticklish part of the feat came in. Then, from this awkward situation, Sophie had to shift her clumsy bulk onto the wall, which was no more than twelve inches wide, while the Doctor changed the ladder.

But in the circus Sophie had been trained to balance herself on small spaces, as well as to climb ladders. And after the Doctor had helped her by leaning down and hoisting her up by the slack of her sealskin jacket, she wiggled herself along the top of the wall beside him and kept her balance as easily as though it were nothing at all.

Then, while Sophie gave a fine imitation of a statue in the moonlight, the Doctor hauled the ladder up after her, swung it over—knocking his own high hat off in the process—and lowered it into the garden once more.

Coming down, Sophie did another of her show tricks: she laid herself across the ladder and slid to the bottom. It was quicker than climbing. And it was lucky she did slide. For the Doctor had hardly lowered the ladder to the lawn when they heard voices in the passage they had left. They had only just gotten into the garden in time.

"Thank goodness for that!" said the Doctor when the sound of footsteps had died away. "A narrow squeak, Sophie! Well, we're safe for the present, anyway. Nobody would dream of looking for you here. Oh, I say, you're lying on the carnations. Come over here onto the gravel. So! Now, shall we sleep in the toolshed or the house?"

"This seems good enough to me," said Sophie, wallowing into the long grass of the lawn. "Let's sleep outdoors."

"No, that will never do," said the Doctor. "Look at all the houses around. If we stay in the garden people could see us out of the top windows when daylight comes. Let's sleep in the toolshed. I love the smell of toolsheds—and then we won't have to break open any doors."

"Nor climb any stairs," said Sophie, humping along toward the shed. "I do hate stairs. Ladders I can manage but stairs are the mischief."

Inside the toolshed they found by the dim light of the moon several old sacks and large quantities of bass-grass. Out of these materials they made themselves two quite comfortable beds.

"My, but it's good to be free!" said Sophie, stretching out

"He lowered the ladder into the garden"

her great, silky length. "Are you sleepy, Doctor? I couldn't stay awake another moment if you paid me."

"Well, go to sleep then," said the Doctor. "I'm going to take a stroll in the garden before turning in."

· The Third Chapter ·

IN THE DESERTED GARDEN

HE Doctor, always fascinated by any kind of a garden, lit his pipe and strolled out of the toolshed into the moonlight. The neglected appearance of the beds and lawns of this deserted property reminded him of his own beautiful home in Puddleby. There were weeds everywhere. John Dolittle could not abide weeds in flower beds. He pulled one or two away from the roots of a rose tree. Further along he found them thicker still, nearly smothering a very fine lavender bush.

"Dear me!" he said, tiptoeing back to the shed for a hoe and a basket. "What a shame to neglect a fine place like this!"

And before long he was weeding away by moonlight like a Trojan—just as though the garden were his own and no danger threatened him within a thousand miles.

"After all," he muttered to himself as he piled the basket high with dandelions, "we are occupying the place—and rent free at that. This is the least I can do for the landlord."

After he had finished the weeding he would have gotten the mower and cut the lawn—only that he was afraid the noise might wake the neighbors.

And when, a week later, the owner of this property rented the place to his aunt, that good lady entirely puzzled her nephew by writing to congratulate him on the way he had had his garden kept!

The Doctor, going back to bed after a hard night's work, suddenly discovered that he was hungry. Remembering the apple trees he had noticed behind a wisteria arbor, he turned back. But no fruit could he find. It had all been gathered or taken by marauding boys. Knowing that he would not be able to move about the garden after daylight came, he then started hunting for vegetables. But in this he had no better luck. So, with the prospect of a foodless day before him tomorrow, he finally went to bed.

In the morning the first thing Sophie said when she woke up was, "My! I've been dreaming about the dear old sea all night. It's given me a wonderful appetite. Is there anything to eat around, Doctor?"

"I'm afraid not," said John Dolittle. "We'll have to go without breakfast—and lunch, too, I fear. I dare not try to get out of here by daylight. As soon as it gets dark, though, I may be able to go by myself and bring you some kippers or something from a shop. But I hope that late tonight they'll have given up hunting for you and that we can both make for the open country and get on our way to the sea."

Well, Sophie was very brave and made the best of it. But as the day wore on they both got ravenously hungry. Somewhere near one o'clock in the afternoon, Sophie suddenly said, "Sh! Did you hear that?"

"No," said the Doctor, who was looking for onions in a corner of the shed. "What was it?"

"It's a dog barking in the passage—the other side of the garden wall. Come out from under the bench and you'll hear it. Goodness! I do hope they're not hunting me with dogs now. The game's up if they do."

The Doctor crawled out from under a potting table, came to the door, and listened. A low, cautious bark reached his ears from over the wall.

"Good Heavens!" he muttered. "That's Jip's voice. I wonder what he wants."

Not far from the shed there was a thick, branchy pear tree standing close to the wall. Making sure no one saw him from the windows of houses overlooking the garden, the Doctor sped across and got behind the tree.

"What is it, Jip?" he called. "Is anything wrong?"

"Let me in," Jip whispered back. "I can't get over the wall."

"How can I?" said the Doctor. "There's no door and I'm afraid the neighbors may see me if I move out in the open."

"Get a rope and tie a basket on the end," whispered Jip. "Then throw it over the wall behind the tree and I'll get in it. When I bark, pull on the rope and haul me up. Hurry! I don't want to be seen around this passage."

Then the Doctor crept back to the toolshed, found a planting line and tied the garden basket on the end of it.

Returning to the cover of the tree, he threw the basket over the wall, but kept the end of the line in his hand.

Presently a bark sounded from the passage and he started hauling in the rope. When the basket reached the top of the wall on the other side Jip's head appeared.

"Keep the rope tight, but tie it to the tree," he whispered. "Then spread your coat out like an apron. I want you to catch some things."

The Doctor did as he was told. And Jip threw down to him the contents of the basket: four ham sandwiches, a bottle of milk, two herrings, a razor, a piece of soap, and a newspaper. Then he threw the empty basket onto the lawn.

"Now catch me," said Jip. "Hold your coat real tight. Ready? One, two, three!"

"My goodness!" said the Doctor as the dog took the flying dive and landed neatly in the coat. "You could perform in the circus yourself."

"I may take it up some day," said Jip carelessly. "Whereabouts in this place have you been living? In the cellar?"

"No. Over there in the toolshed," whispered the Doctor. "Let's slip across quietly and quickly."

A minute later they were safe in the toolshed. Sophie was gulping a herring; and the Doctor was chewing hungrily on a ham sandwich.

"You're a marvel, Jip," said he with his mouth full. "But how did you know we were here—and in need of food? Both of us were just starving."

"Well," said Jip, throwing the seal another herring, "after Sophie got out of the gate the excitement still went on inside the circus. Blossom and his men hunted around all night. Then we decided, from the people's heads popping out of the windows, that the town, too, was pretty much disturbed by the rumpus.

"Too-Too was awfully worried. 'I do hope,' he kept saying, 'that the Doctor has not tried to get out into the country. He'll surely be caught if he has. The thing for him to do for the present is to hide.'

"So all night long we sat up, expecting any minute to see you and Sophie dragged back into the circus. Well, morning came and still you hadn't been captured—and, as far as I know, nobody suspects that you, Doctor, have had anything to do with it. But the circus folk were still searching even when daylight came, and Too-Too kept fussing and

"The dog took the flying dive"

worrying. So I said to him, I said, 'I'll soon tell you if the
Doctor is still in Ashby or not.'

"And I went off on a tour of inspection. It was a damp
morning and a good one for smelling. I made a circular trip
right around the outside of the town. I knew that if you had
left it by any means except flying I could pick up your scent.
But nowhere did I cross the Dolittle trail. So I went back to
Too-Too and I said, 'The Doctor hasn't left Ashby yet—unless he went by balloon.'

" 'Good,' says he. 'Then he's safe in hiding someplace. He's
got wits, has the Doctor—in some things. Now, nose him out

—and come back and tell me where he is. In the meantime I'll have some food got ready for him. Both he and the seal will be hungry. They've neither of them had a thing probably since noon yesterday, and they'll certainly have to stay where they are till late tonight.'

"So then I went smelling around *inside* the town and picked up your incoming trail from where the coach stops. And it led me first, as I expected, by roundabout side streets to the dark passage. But from there, to my surprise, it didn't go on—just stopped dead. Sophie's didn't go on any farther either. Well, I knew you couldn't have crept down a rat hole or flown up in the air; and for a couple of minutes I was absolutely fogged. Then, suddenly, I got a whiff of tobacco smoke coming over the wall—I know the brand you smoke —and I was certain you were in the garden. But, if you ask me, I should say that both of you are pretty fine jumpers."

The Doctor laughed as he started on a second sandwich, and even Sophie, wiping her fishy whiskers with the back of her flipper, smiled broadly.

"We didn't jump the wall, Jip," said John Dolittle. "We used that ladder over there. But how did you get this food here without being seen?"

"It wasn't easy," said Jip, "not by any means. Too-Too and Dab-Dab made up the sandwiches, and we got Sophie's herrings from Higgins' fish pail. The milk was delivered at our wagon by the usual dairyman. Then Too-Too said you'd surely like to see a newspaper—to pass the time—if you had to stay here all day; and I chose *The Morning Gazette*, which is the one we had often seen you reading. Then the white mouse said not to forget your razor and soap because you hated to go without shaving. And we put *them* in. But all this stuff together weighed quite a lot—too much for me to carry in one trip. So I made two, hiding the first load behind

"Sophie smiled"

an ash barrel in the passage till I could fetch the second. On the first journey I got stopped by an old woman—you see, I had the things rolled up in the newspaper, so they wouldn't look so noticeable. 'Oh, my,' said the old lady, 'look at the nice doggie carrying the newspaper for his master! Come here, clever doggie!'

"Well, I gave the old frump the slip and got away from her all right. And then on the second trip I met some more idiots—dog idiots. They caught the scent of the herrings I was carrying for Sophie and started following me in droves. I ran all around the town trying to get away from them and nearly lost the luggage more than once. Finally I put my package down and fought the whole bunch of them . . . No, it wasn't an easy job."

"Goodness!" said the Doctor, finishing his last sandwich and opening the milk. "It's wonderful to have such friends. I'm awfully glad you thought of the razor. I'm getting terribly bristly around the chin . . . Oh, but I haven't any water."

"You must use milk," said Jip. "Steady! Don't drink it all. We thought of that, too, you see."

"Humph," said the Doctor setting down the half-empty bottle. "That's an idea. I never shaved with milk before. Ought to be splendid for the complexion. You don't drink it, Sophie, do you? No. Oh, well, now we're all fixed up."

And he took off his collar and began to shave

After he had finished, Jip said, "Well, I must be leaving, Doctor. I promised them at the caravan I'd come and let them know how everything was going with you as soon as I could. If you don't succeed in getting away tonight I'll be back again the same time tomorrow with some more grub. The townsfolk have pretty much calmed down. But Higgins and Blossom haven't given up the hunt yet by any means. So you will be careful, won't you? You're all safe and snug here. Better stay two days, or even three more, if necessary, rather than run for it too soon and get caught."

"All right, Jip," said the Doctor. "We'll be careful. Thank you ever so much for coming. Remember me to everyone."

"Me, too," said Sophie.

"And tell Too-Too and the rest we are ever so grateful for their help," the Doctor added as he opened the door of the shed.

Then they slipped across to the pear tree again. And after he had climbed into the branches of it, the Doctor poked

Jip, inside the basket, over the wall and let him down on the string into the passage.

Nothing further of excitement happened for some hours. And though, from time to time, they heard the voices of people hunting for them in the passage and the streets around, a pleasant afternoon was spent by the two fugitives, the Doctor reading the paper and Sophie lolling thoughtfully on her bed.

After darkness began to fall John Dolittle could no longer see to read, so he and Sophie took to chatting over plans in low tones.

"Do you think we'll be able to get away tonight, Doctor?" asked Sophie. "Surely, they'll have given up hunting me by then, won't they?"

"I hope so," said the Doctor. "As soon as it's dark I'll go out into the garden and see if I hear anything. I know how anxious you are to be getting along on your trip. But try and be patient."

About half an hour later the Doctor took the ladder and, mounting near the top of the garden wall, he listened long and carefully.

When he came back to Sophie in the toolshed he was shaking his head.

"There are still an awful lot of people moving about in the streets," he said. "But whether they are circus men hunting you, or just ordinary townsfolk walking abroad, I can't make out. We'd better wait a while longer, I think."

"Oh, dear!" sighed Sophie. "Are we never going to get farther than this garden? Poor Slushy! I'm so worried."

And she began to weep softly in the darkness of the shed.

After another hour had gone by the Doctor went out again. This time, just as he was about to climb the ladder, he heard Jip whispering to him on the other side of the wall.

"Doctor, are you there?"

"Yes, what is it?"

"Listen! Higgins and the boss have gone off somewhere with a wagon. Blossom just came and told Matthew to take on some extra jobs with the circus because he wouldn't be back for a while. Too-Too thinks it's a grand chance for you to make a dash for it and get out of the town. Start in an hour, when the circus is in full swing and the men are all busy. Have you got that?"

"Yes, I heard you. Thank you, Jip. All right. We'll leave in an hour." And the Doctor looked at his watch. "Which way did Blossom go?"

"East—toward Grimbledon. Swizzle followed them out a ways and came back and told us. You make for the west. Turn to the left at the end of this passage and then double to the left again at the next corner. It's a dark bystreet and it leads you out onto the Dunwich Road. Once you reach that you'll be all right. There aren't many houses on it and you'll be in the open country in no time. I'm leaving some more sandwiches here in the passage for you. Pick them up on your way out. Can you hear me?"

"Yes, I understand," whispered the Doctor. Then he ran back to the shed with the good news.

Poor Sophie, when she heard they were to leave that night, stood up on her tail and clapped her flippers with joy.

"Now listen," said the Doctor: "if we meet anyone on the street—and we are pretty sure to—you lie down by the wall and pretend you're a sack I'm carrying—that I'm taking a rest, you see. Try and look as much like a sack as you can. Understand?"

"All right," said Sophie. "I'm frightfully excited. See how my flippers are fluttering."

"John Dolittle paused"

Well, the Doctor kept an eye on his watch; and long before the hour had passed he and Sophie were waiting at the foot of the ladder ready and impatient.

Finally, after looking at the time once more, the Doctor whispered, "All right, I think we can start now. Let me go first so I can steady the ladder for you, the way I did before."

But, alas, for poor Sophie's hopes! Just as the Doctor was halfway up, the noise of distant barking, deep-voiced and angry, broke out.

John Dolittle paused on the ladder, frowning. The barking—many dogs baying together—drew nearer.

"What's that?" said Sophie in a tremulous whisper from below. "That's not Jip or any of our dogs."

"No," said the Doctor, climbing down slowly. "There's no mistaking that sound. Sophie, something's gone wrong. That's the baying of bloodhounds—bloodhounds on a scent. And they're coming this way!"

· The Fourth Chapter ·

THE LEADER OF THE BLOODHOUNDS

JIP, after his last conversation with the Doctor over the garden wall, returned to the caravan and his friends, feeling comfortably sure that now everything would go all right.

He and Too-Too were chatting under the table while Dab-Dab was dusting the furniture, when suddenly in rushed Toby, all out of breath.

"Jip," he cried. "The worst has happened! They've got bloodhounds. That's what Blossom and Higgins went off for. There's a man who raises them, it seems, in the next village. They're bringing 'em here in a wagon—six of 'em. I spotted them just as they entered the town over the toll-bridge. I ran behind and tried to speak to the dogs. But with the rattle of the wagon wheels they couldn't hear me. If they put those hounds on Sophie's trail she's as good as caught already."

"Confound them!" muttered Jip. "Where are they now, Toby?"

"I don't know. When I left them they were crossing the marketplace on their way here at a trot. I raced ahead to let you know as quick as I could."

"All right," said Jip, springing up. "Come with me."

And he dashed out into the night.

"They'll try and pick up the trail from the seal's stand," said Jip as the two dogs ran on together across the enclosure. "Perhaps we can meet them there."

But at the stand there were no bloodhounds.

Jip put his nose to the ground and sniffed just once.

"Drat the luck!" he whispered. "They've been here already and gone off on the trail. Listen, there they are, baying now. Come on! Let's race for the passage. We may be in time yet."

And away he sped like a white arrow toward the gate, while poor little Toby, left far behind, with his flappy ears trailing in the wind, put on his best speed to keep up.

Dashing into the passage, Jip found it simply full of men and dogs and lanterns. Blossom was there, and Higgins, and the man who owned the hounds. While the men talked and waved the lamps, the hounds, six great, droopy-jowled beasts, with long ears and bloodshot eyes, sniffed the ground and ran hither and thither about the alley, trying to find where the trail led out. Every once in a while they would lift their noses, open their big mouths, and send a deep-voiced howl rolling toward the moon.

By this time other dogs in the neighborhood were answering their bark from every backyard. Jip ran into the crowded passage, pretending to join in the hunt for scent. Picking out the biggest bloodhound, who, he guessed, was the leader, he got alongside of him. Then, still keeping his eyes and nose to the ground, he whispered in dog language, "Get your duffers out of here. This is the Doctor's business— John Dolittle's."

The bloodhound paused and eyed Jip haughtily.

"Who are you, mongrel?" he said. "We've been set to run

down a seal. Stop trying to fool us. John Dolittle is away on a voyage."

"He's nothing of the kind," muttered Jip. "He's on the other side of that wall—not six feet away from us. He is trying to get this seal down to the sea so she can escape these men with the lanterns—if you idiots will only get out of the way."

"I don't believe you," said the leader. "The last I heard of the Doctor he was traveling in Africa. We must do our duty."

"Duffer! Numbskull!" growled Jip, losing his temper entirely. "I'm telling you the truth. For two pins I'd pull your long ears. You must have been asleep in your kennel the last two years. The Doctor's been back in England over a month. He's traveling with the circus now."

But the leader of the bloodhounds, like many highly trained specialists, was (in everything outside his own profession) very obstinate and a bit stupid. He just simply would not believe that the Doctor wasn't still abroad. In all his famous record as a tracker he had never failed to run down his quarry once he took up a scent. He had a big reputation, and was proud of it. He wasn't going to be misled by every whippersnapper of a dog who came along with an idle tale—no, not he.

Poor Jip was in despair. He saw that the hounds were now sniffing at the wall over which Sophie had climbed. He knew that these great beasts would never leave this neighborhood while the seal was near, and her fishy scent so strong all about. It was only a matter of time before Blossom and Higgins would guess that she was in hiding beyond the wall and would have the old house and garden searched.

While he was still arguing, an idea came to Jip. He left the knot of bloodhounds and nosed his way carelessly down to the bottom of the passage. The air was now simply full of barks and yelps from dogs of every kind. Jip threw back his head and pretended to join in the chorus. But the message he shouted was directed over the wall to the Doctor:

"These idiots won't believe me. For heaven's sake tell 'em you're here—*Woof! Woof! WOO—!*"

And then still another doggish voice, coming from the garden, added to the general noise of the night. And this is what it barked:

"It is I, John Dolittle. Won't you please go away? *Wow! Woof! Wow-ow!*"

At the sound of that voice—to Blossom and Higgins no different from any of the other yelps that filled the air—the noses of all six bloodhounds left the ground and twelve long ears cocked up, motionless and listening.

"By ginger!" muttered the leader. "It is he! It's the great man himself."

"What did I tell you?" whispered Jip, shuffling toward him. "Now lead these men off toward the south—out of the town, quick—and don't stop running till morning."

Then the dog trainer saw his prize leader suddenly double around and head out of the passage. To his delight, the others followed his example.

"All right, Mr. Blossom," he yelled, waving his lantern. "They've got the scent again. Come on, follow 'em, follow 'em! They're going fast. Stick to 'em! . . . Run!"

Tumbling over one another to keep up, the three men hurried after the hounds; and Jip, to help the excitement in the right direction, joined the chase, barking for all he was worth.

"They've turned down the street to the south," shouted the owner. "We'll get your seal now, never fear. Ah, they're good dogs! Once they take the scent they never go wrong. Come on, Mr. Blossom. Don't let 'em get too far away."

And in a flash the little dark passage, which a moment before was full and crowded, was left empty in the moonlight.

Poor Sophie, weeping hysterically on the lawn, with the Doctor trying to comfort her, suddenly saw the figure of an owl pop up onto the garden wall.

"Doctor! Doctor!"

"Yes, Too-Too. What is it?"

"Now's your chance! The whole town's joined the hunt. Get your ladder. Hurry!"

And two minutes later, while the hounds, in full cry, led Blossom and Higgins on a grand steeplechase over hill and dale to the southward, the Doctor led Sophie quietly out of Ashby by the Dunwich Road, toward the westward and the sea.

When Sophie and John Dolittle had traveled down the Dunwich Road as far as where the houses of Ashby ended and the fields of the country began, they both heaved a sigh of relief. What they had been most afraid of while still in the streets was being met by a policeman. The Doctor guessed that Higgins had probably applied to the police station and offered a reward for the return of his lost property. If he had, of course, all the town constables would be very much on the lookout for stray seals.

As they now plodded along the road between hedgerows, the Doctor could tell from Sophie's heavy breathing and very slow pace that even this bit of land travel had already wearied the poor beast. Yet he dared not halt upon the highway.

Spying a copse over in some lonely farming lands to his left, he decided that it would make a good, snug place in which to take a rest. He therefore turned off the road, found

"A steeplechase over hill and dale"

a hole in the hedge for Sophie to crawl through, and led her along a ditch that ran up toward the copse.

Arriving at the little clump of trees and brambles, they found it excellent cover and crawled in. It was the kind of place where no one would be likely to come in a month of Sundays—except perhaps stray sportsmen after rabbits, or children berry-picking.

"Well," said the Doctor, as Sophie flopped down, panting within the protection of dense hawthorns and furze, "so far, so good."

"He found a hole for Sophie to crawl through"

"My!" said Sophie, "but I'm winded. Seals weren't meant for this kind of thing, Doctor. How far do you reckon we've come?"

"About a mile and a half, I should say."

"Good Lord! Is that all? And it's nearly a hundred to the sea! I tell you what I think we ought to do, Doctor; let's make for a river. Rivers always flow to the sea. I can travel in water as fast as a horse can run. But much more of this highroad walking will wear holes in the sole of my stomach. A river's the thing we've got to make for."

"Yes, I think you're right, Sophie. But where to find one? That's the point. If we were anywhere near Puddleby now, I could tell you at once. But I don't know a thing about the geography of these parts. I ought to have remembered to bring a map with me. I don't want to be asking people—not yet, anyway. Because I'm still supposed to be miles away from here, attending to business."

"Well, ask some animal, then," said Sophie.

"Of course!" cried the Doctor. "Why didn't I think of that before? Now, what kind of a beast could best give us the information we want?"

"Oh, any sort of water creature will do."

"I know. We'll ask an otter. Otters are about your nearest relatives in England, Sophie. They travel and hunt in fresh water very much the way you do in salt. Now you stay here and take a good rest, and I'll go off and find one."

It was about one o'clock in the morning when the Doctor returned to the copse. The noise he made entering woke Sophie out of a sound sleep.

With him he had brought a rather unusual animal. In odd, curving, graceful leaps this creature kept bounding up out of the high bracken that carpeted the copse to get a good look at Sophie. He seemed somewhat afraid of her, but very interested.

"Isn't she large, Doctor!" he whispered. "Did you say she was related to us?"

"In a way, yes. Though, strictly speaking, she is a *pinniped*, while your people are *musteloids.*"

"Oh, well, I'm glad of it. She is so clumsy. And look, she hasn't any hind legs—just sort of stubby things. Are you sure she won't bite?"

Finally, the otter was persuaded that Sophie was harm-

less, and drawing close, he talked pleasantly with this other
furred fisherman from foreign parts.

"Now," said the Doctor, "as I have told you, we are anxious to get down to the sea by the quickest and quietest way
possible. And Sophie thinks that the best thing is make for
some stream."

"Humph!" said the otter. "She's quite right, of course. But
you've come to a pretty poor place for waterways. The only
reason I stay in this neighborhood is because there are no
otter hounds here. I live and do my fishing in a few ponds.
They're not much good, but at least I'm not hunted by the
packs. There are no decent rivers in these parts—certainly
none that *she* could swim in to the sea."

"Well, where do you recommend us to go, then?" asked
the Doctor.

"I really don't know," said the otter. "You see, I travel so
little myself. I was born in this district. And my mother
always told me that this was the only safe place left in England for otters to live. And so I've stayed here—my whole
life."

"Well, could you get us some fish, then?" asked Sophie.
"I'm famished."

"Oh, surely," said the otter. "Do you eat carp?"

"I'd eat anything just now," said Sophie.

"All right. Wait a minute till I go down to my pond," said
the otter, and he turned around and bounded out of the
copse.

"Why don't you ask the wild ducks, Doctor?" said the otter. "They travel no end, following the waterways up and
down to the sea, feeding. And they always go by the quietest
streams, where they won't meet people. They could tell
you."

" 'Yes,' said the ducks"

"Yes, I think you're right," said John Dolittle. "But where can I get hold of any?"

"Oh, that's easy. They're always flying by night. Just go up on a hill some place and listen. When you hear them passing overhead, call 'em."

So, leaving Sophie and her fresh-water cousin chatting quietly in the copse, the Doctor climbed up a ridge till he came to a high field, from where he could see the moonlit sky all around him. And after a minute or two he heard, a long way off, a faint quacking and honking—wild ducks on the wing. Presently, high above his head, he could make out a V-shaped cluster of little dots, heading seaward.

Putting his two hands to his mouth, like a trumpet, he sent a call hurtling upward. The cluster paused, broke up, and started flying round in circles, coming downward—cautiously—all the time.

Presently, in the copse Sophie and the otter stopped chatting and listened tensely to the sound of approaching footsteps.

Then the figure of John Dolittle stepped into the hiding place, with a lovely green and blue duck tucked comfortably under each arm.

"Well," said the ducks, after the Doctor had explained the situation to them and asked their advice, "The nearest river big enough to be of any use to a seal is the Kippet. Unfortunately, there are no brooks or anything leading into it from here. To reach the valley of Kippet River you'll have to cross about forty miles of land."

"Humph!" said the Doctor. "That sounds bad."

"Very bad," sighed Sophie, wearily. "Poor Slushy! Such a time I'm taking to get to him. What kind of land is this which we've got to cross?"

"It varies a good deal," said the ducks. "Some of it's hilly; some of it's flat; part of it's standing crops; part of it's heath. It's very mixed traveling."

"Dear me!" groaned Sophie.

"Yes," said the ducks, "it would be easier, as far as the river, if you went by road."

"But don't you see," said the Doctor, "I'm afraid of being met and stopped? That's why we left the Dunwich Road. There are too many people who've heard of our escape around these parts."

"But," said the ducks, "you wouldn't have to go back onto

the Dunwich Road. Listen, if you follow the hedge on westward, it will lead you down onto another road, the old Roman road from Igglesby to Grantchester. Coaches use it, going north and south. You're not likely to meet Ashby folks on that. Well, if you go along that road for about forty miles north you'll come to the Kippet River. The highway crosses it at Talbot's Bridge—just before you enter the town of Grantchester."

"It sounds simple for a good walker," said the Doctor. "But for Sophie it's another matter. Still, I suppose it's the best. Follow the Grantchester Road north as far as Talbot's Bridge, and there take to the river, the Kippet—is that it?"

"That's right," said the ducks. "You can't go wrong, once you reach the road. After you take to the stream you'd better make some more inquiries of other waterfowl because, although the Kippet will lead you to the sea, there are places on it where you must be careful."

"Very good," said the Doctor. "You have been most kind. I thank you."

Then the ducks flew off about their business and John Dolittle looked at his watch.

"It's now two o'clock in the morning," said he. "We have three hours more before daylight comes. Would you prefer, Sophie, to stay here and rest till tomorrow evening, or shall we push on and get as far as we can before dawn?"

"Oh, let's push on," said Sophie.

"All right," said the Doctor, "come along."

While they were making their way along the hedge toward the road, the little otter went off and got Sophie a large meal of fresh fish to help strengthen her for her hard trip. About a mile below, at the end of a long field, he showed them a hole through another hedge, told them the road was just the other side of it, and bade them farewell.

Crawling through, they came out upon a fine highway that stretched away into the night on either hand, wide and well paved.

With a sigh of resignation from Sophie, they turned to the right and set off northward.

· The Fifth Chapter ·

THE PASSENGERS FROM PENCHURCH

O

H, dear! Oh, dear!" said Sophie after they had
traveled for about an hour. "This road is just as hard and
knobby and scrapy as the other one. How far have we come
now?"

"About another mile," said the Doctor.

Sophie began to weep big tears into the white dust of the
road.

"Always 'about another mile'! I'm afraid I'm being a
dreadful nuisance to you, Doctor."

"Oh, not at all," said John Dolittle. "Don't be down-
hearted. We'll do it yet. It'll be easy going once we reach the
river."

"Yes, but we are still thirty-nine miles from that," said
Sophie. "And I'm *so* worn out."

The Doctor looked down at her and saw that, indeed, she
was in a very exhausted state. There was nothing for it but
to halt again.

"Come over here," he said, "off the road—so. Now lie
down in this ditch, where you won't be seen, and take a
rest."

Poor Sophie did as she was told, and the Doctor sat down upon a milestone, thinking hard. Although he was doing his best to cheer Sophie along, it was beginning to look, at this rate, as though they could never get as far as the river.

While he was pondering drearily over the difficulties of the situation, Sophie suddenly said, "What's that noise?"

The Doctor looked up and listened.

"Wagon wheels," he said. "You're quite safe where you are. Just keep still till it passes. You'll never be seen in the ditch."

The rumbling noise drew nearer and presently, around a bend in the road, a light came in sight. Soon the Doctor could see that it was a closed carriage of some kind. As it drew level with him, the driver stopped his horses and called out, "Are you waiting for the coach?"

"Er—er," the Doctor stammered, "—oh, are you the coach?"

"We're one of 'em," said the man.

"Where do you go to?" asked the Doctor.

"We are the local," said the driver; "Penchurch to Anglethorpe. D'yer want to get in?"

While he hesitated over an answer, a wild idea came into the Doctor's head.

"Have you got many passengers?" he asked.

"No, only two—man and his wife—and they're asleep. Plenty o' room inside."

The carriage, lit within by a lamp which shone dimly through drawn curtains, had stopped a little beyond the Doctor's milestone. The driver, from where he sat, could see neither Sophie's hiding place nor the back door of his own coach.

"Are your passengers from these parts?" asked the Doctor, lowering his voice.

"No, we come from Penchurch, I told you. What more would you like to know? If you want to get in, hurry! Can't stay talking all night."

"All right," said the Doctor. "Wait just a second till I get my luggage."

"Want any help?"

"No, no, no! Stay where you are. I can manage."

Then the Doctor slipped behind the end of the coach and opened the door. A man and a woman, with their heads sunk upon their chests, were dozing in the far corner. Leaving the door open, the Doctor ran to the ditch, put his arms around Sophie, and lifted her huge weight bodily in his arms.

"We'll cover part of the ground this way, anyhow," he whispered as he carried her to the coach. "Keep as still and quiet as you can. I'm going to stow you under the seat."

For entering the carriage, whose floor stood high above the level of the road, there were two little iron steps hung below the doorsill. As the Doctor looked in the second time, the passengers were still apparently sleeping. But in trying to mount the steps with his tremendous burden he stumbled noisily. The woman in the corner woke up and raised her head. The Doctor, Sophie's flippers still clinging about his neck, stared, speechless.

"*John!*"

It was Sarah.

Mrs. Dingle fainted with a shriek into her husband's arms. The horses bolted. The Doctor lost his balance entirely. And the coach rattled off into the night, leaving him seated in the road, with Sophie on his lap.

"Heigh-ho!" he sighed, picking himself up wearily. "Of course it would be Sarah! It might have been anyone else in the world, but it *had* to be Sarah. Well, well!"

"He carried her to the coach"

"But what did you mean to do?" asked Sophie. "You could never have gotten me under the seat. There wasn't room there to hide a dog."

"Oh, well, I just acted on the spur of the moment," said the Doctor. "I might have gotten you a few miles on your journey—if I hadn't stumbled and woken Sarah. Bother it! But, you know, Sophie, I think that the coach idea is our best scheme, anyhow. Only we must arrange it a little differently; we must lay our plans with care. In one way it was a good thing it was Sarah. If it had been anyone else who had seen me carrying a seal, they might have talked and set people on our track. But Sarah and her husband are ashamed of my being in the circus business and they won't say anything, we may be sure.

"Now, listen: Over in the east the sky is growing gray—look. It's no use our trying to get farther today. So we'll hide you in those woods down there, and then I'll go on alone to the next village and find out a few things."

So they moved along the highway a short distance to where some pleasant woods bordered the road.

Entering the cover of these preserves, they found a nice place for Sophie to lie hidden. Then, when he had made her comfortable, the Doctor set out down the road just as the cocks in the nearby farms began crowing their first greeting to the morning sun.

After a walk of about two miles he came to a village with a pretty little ivy-covered inn called The Three Huntsmen. Going in he ordered breakfast. He had not had anything to eat since he had left the deserted garden. A very old waiter served him some bacon and eggs in the taproom.

As soon as the Doctor had eaten he lit his pipe and began chatting to the waiter. He found out a whole lot of things about the coaches that ran up and down the Grantchester Road—what the different ones were like to look at, at what hour they were to be expected, which of them were usually crowded, and much more.

Then he left the inn and walked down the street till he came to the few shops the village had. One of these was a general clothier and haberdasher's. The Doctor entered and asked the price of a lady's cloak that was hanging in the window.

"Fifteen shillings and sixpence," said the woman in charge of the shop. "Is your wife tall?"

"My wife?" asked the Doctor, entirely bewildered. "Oh, ah, yes, of course. Well—er—I want it long, anyway. And I'll take a bonnet, too."

"Is she fair or dark?" asked the woman.

"Er—she's sort of medium," said the Doctor.

"There's a nice one here, with red poppies on it," said the woman. "How would she like that?"

"No, that's too showy," said the Doctor.

"Well, they do say them flowery ones is right fashionable up to London just now. How would this do?"

And the woman brought forward a large, plain, black bonnet. "This is very genteel. I wear this kind myself."

"Yes, I'll take that one," said the Doctor. "And now I want a lady's veil—a heavy one, please."

"Oh, mourning in the family?"

"Er—not exactly. But I want it pretty thick—a traveling veil."

Then the woman added a veil to the Doctor's purchases. And with a large parcel under his arm he presently left the shop. Next, he went to a grocery and bought some dried herrings for Sophie—the only kind of fish he could obtain in the village. And about noon he started back down the road.

"Sophie," said John Dolittle, when he reached the seal's hiding place in the woods, "I have a whole lot of information for you, some food, and some clothes."

"Some clothes!" said Sophie. "What would I do with clothes?"

"Wear them," said the Doctor. "You've got to be a lady—for a while, anyhow."

"Great heavens!" grunted Sophie, wiping her whiskers with the back of her flipper. "What for?"

"So as you can travel by coach," said the Doctor.

"But I can't walk upright," cried Sophie, "like a lady."

"I know. But you can sit upright—like a sick lady. You'll

" 'How would this do?' "

have to be a little lame. Any walking there is to be done, I'll carry you."

"But what about my face? It isn't the right shape."

"We'll cover that up with a veil," said the Doctor. "And your hat will disguise the rest of your head. Now, eat this fish I've brought you and then we will rehearse dressing you up. I hear that the Grantchester coach passes by here about eight o'clock—that is, the night one does; and we'll take that because it's less crowded. Now, it's about a four hours' ride to Talbot's Bridge. During all that time you'll have to sit up on your tail and keep still. Do you think you can manage that?"

"I'll try," said Sophie.

"Perhaps you'll have a chance to lie down for a spell if we have the carriage to ourselves part of the way. Much will depend upon how crowded the coach is. It makes three stops between here and Talbot's Bridge. But being a night coach, I don't suppose it will take on many passengers—if we're lucky. Now, let me try these clothes on you and we'll see how you look."

Then the Doctor dressed up Sophie, the performing seal, like a lady. He seated her on a log, put the bonnet on her head, the veil across her face, and the cloak over the rest of her.

After he had gotten her into a human sitting position on the log, it was surprising how natural she looked. In the deep hood of the bonnet her long nose was entirely concealed; and with the veil hung over the front of it, her head looked extraordinarily like a woman's.

"You must be careful to keep your whiskers inside," he said. "That's very important. The cloak is quite long, you see —comes right down to the ground—and while you are seated and it's kept closed in the front it will look quite all right in a dim light. You can keep it drawn together with your flippers—so. Now you look just as though you had your hands folded in your lap—that's the idea, splendid! So long as you can stay that way no one would take you for anything but a lady passenger. . . . Oh, look out! Don't wiggle your head or the bonnet will fall off. Wait till I tie the ribbons under your chin."

"How am I supposed to breathe?" asked Sophie, blowing out the veil in front like a balloon.

"He put the veil across her face"

"Don't do that," said the Doctor. "You're not swimming or coming up for air. You'll get used to it after a while."

"I can't keep very steady this way, Doctor. I'm sitting on the back of my spine, you know. It's an awfully hard position for balancing—much worse than walking on a ladder. What if I should slip down on to the floor of the coach?"

"The seat will be wider than this log and more comfortable. Besides, I'll try to get you into a corner and I'll sit close beside you—so you'll be sort of wedged in. If you feel yourself slipping, just whisper to me and I'll hitch you up into a safer position. You look splendid—really, you do."

Well, after a little more practice and rehearsing the Doctor felt that Sophie could now pass as a lady passenger. And when evening came it found him by the edge of the road, with a heavily veiled woman seated at his side, waiting for the Grantchester coach.

· The Sixth Chapter ·

THE GRANTCHESTER COACH

AFTER they had waited about a quarter of an hour, Sophie said, "I hear wheels, Doctor. And look, there are the lights far down the road."

"Yes," said John Dolittle. "But it isn't the coach we want. That's the Twinborough Express—a green light and a white light. The one we want has two white lights in front. Step back a little further into the shadow of the hedge. Try not to walk on your cloak. You mustn't get it muddy."

A little while after the Twinborough Express had rattled by, along came another.

"Ah!" said the Doctor. "This is ours, the Grantchester coach. Now sit up by the side of the road here and keep perfectly still till I signal the driver. Then I'll lift you in, and let's hope we find a corner seat empty. Is your bonnet on tight?"

"Yes," said Sophie. "But the veil is tickling my nose most awfully. I do hope I don't sneeze."

"So do I," said the Doctor, remembering the cowlike bellow that seals make when they sneeze.

Then John Dolittle stepped out into the middle of the road and stopped the coach. Inside he found three passengers—

117

two men at the far end and an old lady near the door. To his delight, the corner seat opposite the old lady was empty.

Leaving the door open, he ran back and got Sophie and carried her to the coach. The two men at the far end were talking earnestly together about politics. They took little notice as the lame woman was lifted in and made comfortable in the corner seat. But as the Doctor closed the door and sat beside his companion, he noticed that the old lady opposite was very interested in his invalid.

The coach started off, and the Doctor, after making sure that Sophie's feet were not showing below the long cape, got out a newspaper from his pocket. Although the light from the oil lamp overhead was too dim to read by, he spread out the paper before his face and pretended to be deeply absorbed in it.

Presently the old lady leaned forward and tapped Sophie on the knee.

"Excuse me, my dear—" she began in a kindly voice.

"Oh, er—" said the Doctor, looking up quickly. "She doesn't talk—er—that is, not any English."

"Has she got far to go?" asked the old lady.

"To Alaska," said the Doctor, forgetting himself, "er—that is, eventually. This journey, we're only going to Grantchester."

Wishing people would mind their own business, the Doctor plunged again into his paper as though his life depended on his reading every word.

But the kindly passenger was not easily put off. After a moment she leaned forward once more and tapped the Doctor on the knee.

"Is it rheumatics?" she asked in a whisper, nodding toward Sophie. "I noticed that you had to carry her in, poor dear!"

" 'Excuse me, my dear,' she began"

"Er, not exactly," stammered the Doctor. "Her legs are too short. Can't walk. Can't walk a step. Been that way all her life."

"Dear me!" sighed the old lady. "How sad; how very sad!"

"I'm slipping," whispered Sophie behind her veil. "In a minute I'm going to slide onto the floor."

While the Doctor was putting away his newspaper and getting ready to hitch Sophie up higher, the old lady spoke again, "What a nice sealskin coat she's wearing!"

Sophie's knee was sticking out through the cloak.

"Yes. She has to be kept warm," said the Doctor, busily wrapping his invalid up. "Most important."

"She'll be your daughter, I suppose?" asked the old lady.

But this time Sophie spoke for herself. A deep roar suddenly shook the carriage. The tickling of the veil had finally made her sneeze. The Doctor was now standing up, but before he could catch her she had slid down onto the floor between his feet.

"She's in pain, poor thing," said the old lady. "Wait till I get out my smelling bottle. She's fainted. I often do it myself, traveling. And this coach does smell something horrible—fishy like."

Luckily for the Doctor, the old lady then busied herself hunting in her handbag. He was therefore able, while lifting the seal back onto the seat, to place himself in between Sophie and the two men, who were now also showing interest in her.

"Here you are," said the old lady, handing out a silver smelling bottle. "Lift up her veil and hold it under her nose."

"No, thank you," said the Doctor quickly. "All she needs is rest. She's very tired. We'll prop her up snugly in the corner, like this—so. Now, let's not talk, and probably she'll soon drop off to sleep."

Well, finally the poor Doctor got the little old lady to mind her own business and keep quiet. And for about an hour and a half the coach continued on its way without anything further happening. But it was quite clear that the men at the other end were puzzled and curious about his invalid. They kept glancing in her direction and talking together in whispers in a way that make him very uneasy.

Presently the coach stopped at a village to change horses. The driver appeared at the door and told the passengers that if they wished to have supper at the inn (in whose yard they had halted) they had half an hour to do so before they went on.

The two men left the coach, eyeing Sophie and the Doctor as they passed on their way out; and soon the old lady followed their example. The driver had now also disappeared and John Dolittle and his companion had the coach to themselves.

"Listen, Sophie," the Doctor whispered. "I'm getting uneasy about those two men. I'm afraid they suspect that you are not what you pretend to be. You stay here now, while I go in and find out if they're traveling any farther with us."

Then he strolled into the inn. In the passage he met a serving maid and asked the way to the dining room. She showed him an open door with a screen before it a little way down the passage.

"Supper will be served in a minute," she said. "Just walk in and sit down."

"Thank you," said the Doctor. "By the way, do you happen to know who those two men were who came in off the coach just now?"

"Yes, sir," said the maid. "One of them's the county constable and the other's Mr. Tuttle, the mayor of Penchurch."

"Thank you," said the Doctor, and passed on.

Reaching the screen door, he hesitated a moment before entering the dining room. And presently, he heard the voices of the two men seated at a table within on the other side of the screen.

"I tell you," said one in a low tone, "there's not the least doubt. They're highwaymen, as sure as you're alive. It's an old trick, disguising as a woman. Did you notice the trick veil? As likely as not it's that rogue, Robert Finch himself. He robbed the Twinborough Express only last month."

"I shouldn't wonder," said the other. "And the short, thick

"He heard the voices of two men at a table within"

villain will be Joe Gresham, his partner. Now, I'll tell you
what we'll do. After supper let's go back and take our seats
as though we suspected nothing. Their plan, no doubt, is to
wait till the coach is full and has reached a lonely part of the
road. Then they'll hold up the passengers—money or your
life!—and get away before the alarm can be raised. Have
you got your traveling pistols?"

"Yes."

"All right, give me one. Now, when I nudge you—you tear
off the man's veil and hold a pistol to his head. I'll take care

of the short one. Then we'll turn the coach about, drive back, and lodge them in the village jail. Understand?"

While the Doctor was still listening, the maid came down the passage again, with a tray full of dishes, and touched him on the back.

"Go in, sir," she said, "and sit down. I'm just going to serve supper."

"No, thank you," said the Doctor. "I'm not really hungry. I think I'll go out into the air again."

Luckily, on reaching the yard, he found it deserted. The horses had been taken out of the shafts and put into the stable. The new ones had not yet been hitched up to the coach. The Doctor sped across the yard and opened the door.

"Sophie," he whispered, "come out of that. They think we're highwaymen in disguise. Let's get away—quick!—while the coast is clear."

Hoisting the seal's huge weight in his arms, the Doctor staggered out of the yard with her. On account of the lateness of the hour there was no one in the road. All was still and quiet but for the rattle of dishes from the inn kitchen and the noise of washing from the stables.

"Now," said he, putting her down, "we haven't far to go. See, this place is the last in the village. Once we reach those fields and get beyond the hedge we should be all right. I'll go ahead and find a place to get through, and you follow along as quick as you can. Give me your cloak and bonnet—that's it. Now you can travel better."

A few minutes later they were safe behind a high hedge, resting in the long grass of a meadow.

"My!" sighed Sophie, stretching herself out. "It's good to be rid of that wretched cloak and veil. I don't like being a lady a bit."

"That was a narrow escape," said the Doctor. "It's a good thing I went in and overheard those men talking. If we had gone on with them in the coach we'd have been caught for sure."

"Aren't you afraid they'll come hunting for us?" asked Sophie.

"Oh, maybe. But they'll never look for us here. They take us for highwaymen, you see. And by the time they discover our escape they'll probably think we've gone miles. We'll wait here till the coach passes, and then we needn't worry."

"Well," said Sophie, "even if we are safe it doesn't seem to me we are much better off than we were before."

"But we're this much farther on our way," said the Doctor. "Have patience. We'll do it yet."

"How far have we come now?" asked Sophie.

"That village was Shottlake," said the Doctor. "We've got only eighteen miles more to do to reach Talbot's Bridge."

"Well, but how are we going to travel? I can't walk it, Doctor; I simply can't—not eighteen miles."

"Shh! Don't speak so loud," whispered John Dolittle. "They may be snooping around somewhere, looking for us. We'll find a way—don't worry. And once we reach the river, the worst will be over. We must first wait till the coach goes by, though, before we can stir."

"Poor Slushy!" murmured Sophie, looking up at the moon. "I wonder how he's getting on. . . . Will you try to take another coach, Doctor?"

"No. I think we'd better not. They may leave word at the inn and drivers will be on the lookout for a woman of your description."

"Well, I hope they don't find us here," said Sophie. "It doesn't seem to me we're very well concealed. Good heavens! Listen—a footstep!"

The place where they lay was the corner of a pasture field. Besides the hedge that hid them from the road there was another, on their right, dividing their field from the next. Behind this they now heard a heavy footstep passing up and down.

"Keep still, Sophie!" whispered the Doctor. "Don't move an inch."

Presently the top branches of the hedge began to sway and the crackling of twigs reached their ears. "Doctor," said Sophie in a frightened whisper, "they've discovered us. There's someone trying to get through the hedge!"

For a moment or two the Doctor was undecided whether to keep still or to run for it. He thought at first that if it were someone out looking for them he might not know exactly where they were anyway, and would, perhaps, if they kept quiet, go to some other part of the hedge easier to pass through.

But the crackling of branches grew louder—only a few feet away from them. Whoever it was, he seemed determined to enter the field at that place. So, with a whispered word to Sophie, the Doctor sprang up and started off, running across the meadow, with the poor seal flopping along at his side.

On and on they went. Behind them they heard a crash as the hedge gave way, and the heavy footsteps beating the ground in pursuit.

From the sound the pursuer, whoever he was, was gaining on them. And presently the Doctor, fearing that as highwaymen they might be fired upon without warning, turned to look back.

And there, lumbering along behind them, was an old, old plow horse!

"It's all right, Sophie," panted the Doctor halting. "It isn't a man at all. We've had our run for nothing. Good lord, but I'm blown!"

The horse, seeing them stop, slowed down to a walk and came ambling toward them in the moonlight. He seemed very decrepit and feeble; and when he came up Sophie saw with great astonishment that he was wearing spectacles.

"Heavens!" cried the Doctor. "It's my old friend from Puddleby. Why didn't you call to me instead of chasing us across country? We expected you to shoot us in the back any minute."

"Is that John Dolittle's voice I hear?" asked the old horse, peering close into the Doctor's face.

"Yes," said the Doctor. "Can't you see me?"

"Only very mistily," said the plow horse. "My sight's been getting awful bad the last few months. I saw fine for quite a while after you gave me the spectacles. Then I got sold to another farmer, and I left Puddleby to come here. One day I fell on my nose while plowing, and after I got up my spectacles didn't seem to work right at all. I've been almost blind ever since."

"Let me take your glasses off and look at them," said the Doctor. "Perhaps you need your prescription changed."

Then John Dolittle took the spectacles off the old horse and, holding them up to the moon, peered through them, turning them this way and that.

"Why, good gracious!" he cried. "You've got the lenses all twisted. No wonder you couldn't see! That right glass I gave you is quite a strong one. Most important to have them in proper adjustment. I'll soon set them right for you."

"I did take them to the blacksmith who does my shoes," said the old horse as the Doctor started screwing the glasses around in the frames. "But he only hammered the rims and made them worse than ever. Since I was brought to Shott-

"John Dolittle peered through them"

lake I couldn't come to you about them and, of course, our local vet doesn't understand horses' glasses."

"There, now," said the Doctor, putting the spectacles back on his old friend's nose. "I've fixed them tight, so they can't turn. I think you'll find them all right now."

"Oh, my, yes," said the old horse, a broad smile spreading over his face as he looked through them. "I can see you as plain as day. Goodness! How natural you look—big nose, high hat, and all! The sight of you does me good. Why, I can see the very blades of grass by moonlight! You've no idea what an inconvenience it is to be shortsighted, if you're a horse. You spend most of your grazing time spitting out the wild garlic that you chew by accident. . . . My, oh, my! You're the only animal doctor there ever was!"

PART III

· The First Chapter ·

THE HIGHWAYMAN'S DOUBLE

IS he a decent fellow, this farmer you're working for now?" asked the Doctor, seating himself in the grass of the meadow.

"Oh, yes," said the old horse. "He means well. But I haven't done much work this year. He's got a younger team for plowing. I'm sort of pensioned off—only do odd jobs. You see, I'm getting pretty old—thirty-nine, you know."

"Are you, indeed?" said the Doctor. "You don't look it— nothing like it. Thirty-nine! Well, well! Yes, to be sure, now I recollect. You had your thirty-sixth birthday the same week I got you your spectacles. You remember the garden party we gave for you—in the kitchen garden—when Gub-Gub overate himself with ripe peaches?"

"Very well, I do. Ah, those were the days! Good old Pud-dleby! But what's this animal you have with you," asked the plow horse as Sophie moved restlessly in the grass, "a bad-ger?"

"No, that's a seal. Let me introduce you: this is Sophie, from Alaska. We're escaping from the circus. She has to go back to her country on urgent business, and I'm helping her get to the sea."

"Sh!" said Sophie. "Look, Doctor, there's the coach going by."

"Thank goodness for that!" murmured John Dolittle as the lights disappeared down the road.

"You know," said he, turning to the old horse again, "we've had a hard time getting even this far. Sophie has to keep concealed, and she can't walk much. We are making for the Kippet River, at Talbot's Bridge. We came by coach up to Shottlake, but we had to leave it. We were just wondering how we could continue our journey when you scared the life out of us behind that hedge."

"You want to get to Talbot's Bridge?" said the old horse. "Well, that should be easy. Listen you see that barn up on the skyline? Well, there's an old wagon in it. There's no harness but there's plenty of ropes. Let's run up there, and you can hitch me between the shafts, put your seal in the wagon, and we'll go."

"But you'll get into trouble," said the Doctor, "taking your farmer's wagon off like that."

"My farmer will never know," said the old horse, grinning behind his spectacles. "You leave the gate on the latch as we go out, and I'll bring the wagon back and put it where we found it."

"But how will you get out of your harness alone?"

"That's easy. If you knot the ropes the way I tell you, I can undo them with my teeth. I won't be able to take you the whole way because I couldn't get back in time to put the wagon up before daylight comes. But I've got a friend about nine miles down the Grantchester Road, on the Redhill Farm. He gets put out to graze nights, like me. He'll take you the rest of the way. It'll be easy for him to get back to his place before anyone's about."

"Old friend," said the Doctor, "you have a great head. Let's hurry and get on our way."

Then they climbed the hill to the barn. Inside they found an old wagon. The Doctor dragged it out. Then, getting down some ropes that hung coiled against the wall, he rigged up a kind of harness, with the help of an old collar, which he found thrown up in the manger. And when the plow horse had set himself between the shafts, John Dolittle hitched him up, being careful to make all the knots exactly the way he was told.

Then he lifted Sophie into the wagon and they started off down the meadow toward the gate.

As they were going out the Doctor said, "But suppose anyone should meet me driving a wagon in a high hat? Wouldn't it seem sort of suspicious? . . . Oh, look: There's a scarecrow in the next field. I'll borrow his hat."

"Bring the whole scarecrow with you," the old horse called after him as the Doctor started off. "I'll need something as a dummy driver when I'm coming back. Folks would stop me if they thought I was straying around the country without a driver."

"All right," said the Doctor and he ran off.

In a few minutes he came marching back with the scarecrow on his shoulder. Then he set the gate on the latch so the old horse could push it open on his return, threw the scarecrow up into the wagon, and climbed in himself.

Next, he took the scarecrow's tattered hat and put it on his own head in place of his high one. Then he got into the driver's seat, lifted the rope reins in his hands, called "Geeup!" to his old friend between the shafts, and they started off.

"You better keep your cloak and bonnet ready to slip on, Sophie," said he. "Somebody might ask for a ride. And if we

"He rigged up a kind of harness"

are compelled to give anyone a lift you'll have to be a lady again."

"I'd sooner be almost anything in the world than a lady," sighed Sophie, remembering the tickling veil. "But I'll do it if you say so."

Thus, driving his own farm-wagon coach, with a scarecrow and a seal for passengers, John Dolittle successfully completed the next stage in his strange journey. They passed very few people, and no one asked for a ride. They had one anxious moment, however, when a gentleman armed with pistols in his saddle holsters galloped up on a very fine

"Came marching back with the scarecrow on his shoulder"

horse and asked if they had seen anything of a man and a veiled woman along the road.

The Doctor, sitting on top of Sophie, leaned on the side of his wagon, with his scarecrow hat pulled well down over his eyes.

"I saw a couple getting into a field a few miles back," he said, trying to talk like a yokel. "But I reckon they be a long ways from there by now."

"That'll be they, sure enough," said the man putting spurs to his horse: "Finch and Gresham, the highwaymen. They boarded the coach below Shottlake. But they got away before we could arrest them. Never mind, we'll get 'em yet. Good night!"

And he galloped off down the road.

"Poor Mr. Finch!" said the Doctor, as the old horse moved on. "I'm afraid we are not improving his reputation for him."

"It's a good thing I got you away from Shottlake," said the old horse. "I reckon that fellow will set the whole country busy hunting for you now."

"Their hunting won't do us any harm back at Shottlake," said the Doctor. "Good thing if they're kept busy. But I hope you don't get into trouble on your return to the farm."

"No, I don't suppose so," said the old horse. "Even if I'm seen they'll never guess how I got hitched up. Don't bother about me. I'll manage."

A little further on the plow horse stopped.

"This is Redhill Farm on the right," said he. "Wait till I call Joe."

Then he went close to the hedge beside the road and neighed softly. Presently there was a scampering of hoofs and his friend, a much younger horse, poked his head over the hawthorns.

"I've got John Dolittle here," whispered the plow horse. "He wants to get to Talbot's Bridge in a hurry. Can you take him?"

"Why, certainly," said the other.

"You'll have to use a wagon of your own," said the plow horse. "I must get mine back to the barn before my farmer wakes up. Got a cart or something anywhere about the place?"

"Yes, there's a trap up in the yard. It'll be faster than a wagon. Come over this side of the hedge, Doctor, and I'll show you where it is."

Then, hurrying lest daylight overtake them, they made the exchange. Madam Sophie was transferred from a farm wagon to a smart trap. The old plow horse, after an affectionate farewell from the Doctor, started back with his own wagon, driven by his scarecrow propped up on the front seat. At the same time John Dolittle and Sophie were carried at a good, swift pace in the opposite direction, toward the Kippet River.

On arriving at his own farm, the old horse found everyone in a great state of excitement. People were rushing wildly up and down the fields with lanterns. The scarecrow had been missed; so had the old wagon; so had the old horse. The farm laborers were following the wheel tracks across the meadow. As soon as the plow horse reached the gate he was surrounded by a mob with lamps and guns, all guessing and advising and chattering at once.

In the meantime the Doctor and Sophie, in their trap, were spanking along the road in the direction of Talbot's Bridge. And, although the horseman (he was the county constable's assistant) galloped after them as hard as he could, he never overtook them, with the good start they had gained.

On reaching the river, the Doctor lifted Sophie out of the trap and dropped her over the bridge into the stream. Telling the Redhill horse to go back to his farm by a different way, lest he be met by the man again, John Dolittle leapt off the parapet of the bridge onto the bank. Then, while he ran along the stream beside her, Sophie, with gurgles of delight, plunged and darted through the river, catching all the fish she wanted on the way.

· The Second Chapter ·

TO THE SEA BY RIVER

AS they had expected, John Dolittle and Sophie now found that the worst part of their troublesome traveling was over. If they met anyone on the banks of the stream Sophie just ducked underwater till the danger was past, while the Doctor pretended he was fishing, with a willow wand for rod and a piece of string for line.

They still had a long way to go. The journey north to Talbot's Bridge, you see, had not brought them any nearer to the coast.

The country through which the Kippet flowed was pleasant and sometimes it passed close by a farm, where cattle drank. At these places the travelers would either wait till nightfall, lest they be seen, or if the depth of the river permitted, Sophie would do her swimming underwater while the Doctor would go around by the roads and meet her farther down.

While the going was, for the most part, easy for a seal, it was by no means always simple for the Doctor. The hundreds of hedges he had to get through, the walls he had to climb, the bogs he had to cross made his part of the journey a hard and slow one. Sophie had to slacken her pace constantly and do a lot of loitering and waiting in order that he might keep up with her.

"Look here, Doctor," said she, about the middle of the second day when John Dolittle was resting on the bank, "it doesn't seem to me there is really any need for you to come farther. This going is so easy for me I can do the rest of the journey by myself, can't I?"

"I think not," said the Doctor, lying back and gazing up at the willows over his head. "We don't know yet what sort of difficult places the river may run you into before it reaches the sea. We had better consult some other waterfowl, as the ducks said we should, before we go farther."

Just at that moment a pair of fine bitterns flew down into the stream not far away and started feeding. The Doctor called them and they came up at once to his side.

"Would you please tell us," said John Dolittle, "how much farther the river runs before it reaches the sea?"

"Counting all the bends and wiggles," said the bitterns, "about sixty miles."

"Dear me!" said the Doctor. "Then we are barely halfway yet. What kind of country does it pass through? This seal wishes to swim all the way to the coast, and we must avoid having people see her on the way."

"Well," said the birds, "you will have plain sailing for another ten miles yet. But after that there are several places pretty dangerous for a seal to travel. The first one is Hobbs's Mill. It's a water mill, you understand, and the stream is dammed up with a high dam, a weir, and a big waterwheel. She'll have to leave the water at Hobbs's Mill and join it again below."

"All right," said the Doctor, "we can do that, I imagine. Then, what's the next trouble?"

"The next is a town. It isn't a large one, but it has machinery buildings in it on the riverbank. And the river is made to run into pipes to turn these machines, and if your seal went floating down the pipes she'd get all mixed up in the machinery."

"I understand," said the Doctor. "Then we'll have to go around the town by land—after dark."

"Go around to the *right,*" said the bitterns—"to the northward. On the other side the machinery-men's houses spread out a long way.

"After that you'll be all right till you get very nearly to the sea. But there you will meet with another town—a port. Your seal can't possibly swim through that town because the river flows over many little waterfalls and rapids right where the houses and bridges are thickest. So as soon as you come in sight of the port you had better leave the stream again, and make for the seashore at some lonely place to the north of it. You won't have far to go, but you'll have to do some stiff climbing, for the coast thereabouts is all high cliffs. If you get safely past the port without being caught your troubles will be over."

"Well, thank you very much," said the Doctor. "This knowledge will be most helpful to us. Now I think we had better be getting on our way."

Then after wishing John Dolittle good luck, the bitterns went back to their feeding, and the Doctor proceeded along the bank with Sophie swimming in the river. They reached Hobbs's Mill just as evening was coming on. As soon as the Doctor had explored around the buildings to see that all was quiet and nobody abroad, Sophie got out of the stream and hobbled across a couple of meadows and joined the river below the millrace on the other side. There they waited till

"They reached Hobbs's Mill just as evening
was coming on"

the moon rose, and soon, with sufficient light for the Doctor
to see his way along the shore, they went on again.

Coming in sight of the machinery town of which the bitterns had spoken, John Dolittle left Sophie with orders to
duck underwater if anyone should pass that way, and went
forward into the town to explore and get some food for
himself.

Although most of the shops were shut at this hour, he
managed to buy some sandwiches and fruit at a hotel. In
making these purchases he noticed that his supply of money

was getting very low. Indeed, he had only just enough to pay for what he had bought. However, never having bothered much about money, this did not disturb him. And after spending his last twopence to get his boots cleaned—they were frightfully muddy from all this boggy walking—he proceeded to explore a way for Sophie to come around the town by land.

The journey she would have to make on foot proved to be quite a long one. But the Doctor found a way over a chain of ponds, waterlogged meadows, and a little brook that ran into the Kippet about two miles the other side of the town.

By the time he returned to Sophie the night was nearly passed, and they had to hurry to reach the river again before daylight came.

With Sophie safely back in the stream, John Dolittle decided he had better take a little sleep before going on. Sophie, too, was pretty weary, in spite of her anxiety to push on with all possible speed. So, asking a little moorhen, who had her nest in the bank of the stream to mount guard and wake them on the approach of danger, they both took a nap —Sophie sleeping in the water, with her head poked out onto a stump, and the Doctor propped against a willow tree on the shore.

The sun was high in the heavens when he awoke to find the moorhen plucking at his sleeve.

"There's a farmer driving a team across the meadow," whispered the little bird. "He'll come right by here. He might not take any notice of you, but Sophie he couldn't miss. Get her to stick her head under the water. She's snoring like a foghorn, and I can't wake her up."

After the Doctor had made Sophie disappear beneath the water, and the danger of discovery was past, they started off once more and traveled all day and the following night toward the sea.

Gradually the landscape changed and finally, on the evening of the next day, they saw the lights of the seaport town twinkling in the distance. The land either side of it sloped upward to cliffs overlooking the Bristol Channel.

A little farther down the stream roads ran either side of the river, presumably going into the town. Along these, every once in a while, coaches and carriages passed them on their way to the port.

Feeling that it would be unwise to go farther by water, they now left the stream for the last time and hit out across country.

The Doctor made Sophie keep her bonnet on, and he had her cloak ready to throw over her at any minute because there were many roads to cross and farmhouses to pass upon the way.

About a mile had to be covered before they would reach the top of the long slope and come in sight of the sea beyond the cliffs. Picking out a line which would miss most of the barns on the downs, they proceeded steadily and slowly forward. On this upland country they met with many stone walls. And though they were low enough for the Doctor to jump, they were too much for Sophie to manage and the Doctor had to lift her over.

She did not complain, but the uphill going was telling on her terribly. And when at last they came to a level stretch at the top, and the wind from the Channel beat in their faces, Sophie was absolutely exhausted and unable to walk another step.

The distance now remaining to the edge of the cliffs was not more than a hundred yards. Hearing the voices of people singing in a house near by, the Doctor began to fear that they might yet be discovered—even with the end of their

"He threw Sophie into the Bristol Channel!"

long trip in sight. So with poor Sophie in a state of utter
collapse, he decided there was nothing for it but to carry her
the remainder of the journey.

As he put the cloak about her he saw the door of the house
open and two men came out. Hurriedly he caught the seal
up in his arms and staggered with her toward the edge of
the cliffs.

"Oh," cried Sophie when they had gone a few yards, "look,
the sea! How fresh and nice it sparkles in the moonlight.
The sea, the sea at last!"

"Yes, this is the end of your troubles, Sophie," the Doctor panted as he stumbled forward. "Give my regards to the herd when you reach Alaska."

At the edge John Dolittle looked straight downward to where the deep salt water swirled and eddied far below.

"Good-bye, Sophie," he said with what breath he had left. "Good-bye, and good luck!"

Then, with a last tremendous effort, he threw Sophie over the cliff into the Bristol Channel.

Turning and twisting in the air, the seal sped downward—her cloak and bonnet, torn off her by the rushing air, floating more slowly behind. And as she landed in the water the Doctor saw the white foam break over her, and the noise of a splash gently reached his ears.

"Well," he said, mopping his brow with a handkerchief, "thank goodness for that! We did it, after all. I can tell Matthew that Sophie reached the sea and I *didn't* go to jail."

Then a cold shiver ran down his spine. A heavy hand had grasped his shoulder from behind.

· The Third Chapter ·

SIR WILLIAM PEABODY, J. P.

JOHN DOLITTLE, turning about slowly, found a large man grasping his collar. He wore some kind of a sailorlike uniform.

"Who are you?" asked the Doctor.

"Coastguard," said the man.

"What do you want? Let go of my coat."

"You're arrested."

"What for?"

"Murder."

While the Doctor was still trying to recover from his astonishment he saw more people coming across the downs from the lonely house that he had already noticed. When they came close he saw they were two men and a woman.

"Have you got him, Tom?"

"Yes. Caught 'im right in the act."

"What was it?"

"A woman," said the coastguard. "I grabbed him just as he threw her over the cliff. Jim, you run down to the station and get the boats out. You may be in time to save her yet. But I doubt it. I'll take him along to the quod. You come on down there or send me word if you find anything."

"It'll be his wife," said the woman, peering at the Doctor in awe and horror. "Murdered his wife! You Bluebeard! He ought to be still more ashamed of 'isself," said the woman— "much more than if he'd been brought up to such habits— pore creature!" (She gazed over the edge of the cliff with a shudder.) "I wonder will they find 'er. Seems to me almost as though I could see something floating on the water down there. Pore creature! Well, that's the end of her troubles. Maybe she's better off than she was, married to him, the brute!"

"It wasn't my wife," said the Doctor sullenly.

"Who was it, then?" asked the coastguard. "It was some woman—'cause I seen you carrying her in your arms."

To this the Doctor decided, after a moment of thought, to say nothing. Now that he was arrested he would probably have to admit in the end that it was Sophie he had thrown into the sea. But until he was compelled in court to tell the whole story it seemed wiser to keep silence.

"Who was it?" the man repeated.

Still the Doctor said nothing.

"It was his wife all right," said the woman. "He has a wicked eye. I'll bet he has five or six wives stowed away somewhere—waiting for their doom, pore things."

"Well, he don't have to answer," said the coastguard. "It's my duty to warn you," he said very grandly, turning to the Doctor, "that anything you say may be used in evidence against you. Now let's go down to the courthouse."

Fortunately for the Doctor it was by this time well on into the early hours of the morning. And when after crossing the downs they finally made their way into the town they found the streets deserted. The woman had not accompanied them. And the Doctor and his coastguard reached the courthouse without meeting a single soul.

" 'You Bluebeard!' "

Just as they were about to enter the police station next door, Jim, the other coastguard man, ran up and joined his companion, with Sophie's wet cloak on his arm and her bonnet in his hand.

"We couldn't find the body, Tom," said he, "but these clothes was floating at the foot of the cliff. I've left Jerry Bulkley in the boat still searching. I brought these down to you 'cause I thought you might want 'em."

"Yes, they'll be needed in evidence," said the other, taking the things from him. "Better go back and carry on with the search. I'll come and join you as soon as I've got the prisoner locked up."

Then the poor Doctor was taken into the police station; and after his name and various particulars about him were written down in a big book, he was placed in a little stone cell with some bread and water and left to his meditations.

As the noise of the clanging door and rattling bolts died away, John Dolittle noticed the gray light of dawn creeping in at a little barred window at his elbow.

"Heigh-ho!" he sighed, gazing around the bare stone walls. "Jail again! I congratulated myself too soon. I wonder, was Matthew ever in *this* prison."

Where the morning sun fell in a patch upon the wall he noticed some letters and signs scratched in the stone by former prisoners. He crossed the cell and examined them. Among them he found a very badly made "M. M."

"Yes," he said, "Matthew's been here, too. Seems proud of it. Well, well—it's a funny world."

Picking up the loaf that had been provided for him, he broke it in half and ate a couple of mouthfuls. He was very hungry.

"What good bread!" he murmured. "Quite fresh. I must ask the jailer where he gets it. The bed isn't bad either," he added, punching the mattress. "I think I'll take a nap. Haven't had a decent sleep in I don't know how long."

Then he took his coat off, rolled it up for a pillow, and lay down.

And when, about ten o'clock in the morning, the superintendent of police entered with a tall white-haired gentleman they found the prisoner stretched on his cot snoring loudly.

"Humph!" murmured the old gentleman in a low voice. "He doesn't look very dangerous, does he, Superintendent?"

"He found a badly made 'M. M.'"

"Ah," said the other, shaking his head, "it only shows you, Sir William, what a life of crime will do. Fancy being able to sleep like that after throwing his poor wife into the sea!"

"Well, leave us alone for a little while," said the older man. "Come back in about a quarter of an hour. And, by the way, you need not mention my visit here to anyone—not for the present."

"Very good, Sir William," said the superintendent. And he went out, locking the door behind him.

Then the white-haired old gentleman went over to the cot

and stood looking down a moment into the Doctor's peaceful face.

Presently he shook the sleeper gently by the shoulder.

"Dolittle," he said. "Here—John, wake up!"

Slowly the Doctor opened his eyes and raised himself on his elbow.

"Where am I?" he said drowsily. "Oh, yes, of course, in jail."

Then he stared at the man who stood beside him. And at last a smile spread over his face.

"Heavens above! It's Sir William Peabody," said he. "Well, well, William! What on earth brings you here?"

"I might still more reasonably ask you how *you* come to be here," said the visitor.

"My goodness!" murmured the Doctor. "It must be fifteen years since I've seen you. Let me see: The last time was when we both got pretty angry—you remember?—arguing for and against fox hunting. Have you given it up yet?"

"No," said Sir William. "I still hunt two days a week. That's all I can manage now with my court duties and other things. They made me a Justice of the Peace about five years ago."

"Well, it ought to be stopped," said the Doctor, with great earnestness, "altogether. You can say what you like, but the fox is not given a square deal. One fox against dozens of dogs! Besides, why should he be hunted? A fox has his rights, the same as you and I have. It's absurd: A lot of grown men on horses, with packs of hounds, roaring across country after one poor little wild animal."

The old gentleman sat down on the bed beside the Doctor, threw back his head, and laughed.

"Same old Dolittle," he chuckled. "Did anyone ever see the like? In jail, charged with murder, the first thing he does when I come to see him is try and open a discussion about fox hunting. Ever since I've known you, John—even when you were a scrubby little boy at school studying beetles under a magnifying glass—you've been the same. Listen, I haven't come here to argue about the rights of foxes. As I told you, I'm a J. P. You're due to appear before me for examination in about an hour. What I want to hear is your version of this charge that is brought against you. You are accused of murdering your wife. I happened to notice your name on the police book. From what I remember of you, I can well understand your killing any woman who was mad enough to marry you. But the part I don't believe is that you ever had a wife. What's it all about? They tell me you were seen throwing a woman into the sea."

"It wasn't a woman," said the Doctor.

"What was it then?"

The Doctor looked down at his boots and fidgeted like a schoolboy caught doing something wrong.

"It was a seal," he said at last, "a circus seal dressed up as a woman. She wasn't treated properly by her keepers. And she wanted to escape, to get back to Alaska and her own people. So I helped her. I had the very dickens of a time bringing her across country all the way from Ashby. I had to disguise her as a woman so we could travel without arousing suspicion. And the circus folk were out after me. Then just as I got her here to the coast and was throwing her into the sea so she could swim back to her native waters, one of your coastguard men saw me and put me under arrest—what are you laughing about?"

Sir William Peabody, who had been trying to suppress a smile throughout the Doctor's story, was now doubled up with merriment.

"As soon as they said it was your wife," he gurgled when

he had partly recovered, "I knew there was something fishy about it. And there was, all right! You do smell terrible."

"Seals have to smell of fish," said the Doctor in an annoyed tone. "And I was compelled to carry her part of the way."

"You'll never grow up, John," said Sir William, shaking his head and wiping the tears of laughter from his eyes. "Now tell me: How far back on this trip of yours were you and the lady you eloped with seen? Because although we can certainly get you out of the charge of wife murder, it may not be so easy to clear you on the charge of stealing a seal. Were you followed down here, do you think?"

"Oh, no. We were not bothered by the circus folk after we got away from Ashby. Then at Shottlake we got taken for highwaymen and caused a little sensation when we traveled by coach. But after that nobody suspected anything till . . . till—"

"Till you threw your ladylove over the cliff," Sir William put in. "Did anyone see you being brought in here?"

"No," said the Doctor. "No one down here knows anything about it except the three coastguardsmen and a woman— the wife of one of them, I suppose. The streets were quite empty when I was brought to the jail."

"Oh, well," said Sir William, "I think we can manage it. You'll have to stay here till I can get the charge withdrawn. Then get away from this part of the country as quick as you can."

"But what about the coastguard folk?" asked the Doctor. "Are they still hunting for the body?"

"No, they've given it up now," said Sir William. "They brought back your victim's cloak and bonnet. That was all they could find. We'll say you were just throwing some old clothes into the sea—which is partly true. When I explain matters to them they won't talk—and even if they do, it isn't likely their gossip will ever reach your circus people. But listen, Dolittle: Do me a favor and don't bring any more menageries down here to throw over our cliffs, will you? It would get hard to explain if you made a habit of it. Besides, you'll spoil the circus business. Now you stay here till I've fixed things up officially; and as soon as they let you out, get away from this district. Understand?"

"All right," said the Doctor. "Thank you. But listen, Will, about that fox hunting . . . Supposing you were in the fox's—"

"No," said Sir William, rising. "I refuse to reopen the argument now, John. I hear the superintendent coming back. We have too many foxes in this country. They need to be kept down."

"Quite a nice prison you have here, Will," said the Doctor as the superintendent opened the door. "Thanks for calling."

When Sir William and the superintendent had disappeared the Doctor fell to walking up and down his cell for exercise. He began to wonder how things were getting on with his household in his absence. And he was still thinking over the animals' idea of a reformed circus when, about half an hour later, a police sergeant appeared at the door, extraordinarily polite and gracious.

"The superintendent presents his compliments, Doctor," he said, "and apologizes for the mistake that was made. But it was not our department's fault. It was the coastguards who made the arrest. Very stupid of them, very. The charge is now withdrawn, Sir, and you are free to go whenever you wish."

"Thank you," said the Doctor. "I think I'll go now. It's a nice prison you have here—almost the best I was ever in. Tell the superintendent he needn't apologize. I've had a most

" 'Excellent bread you have here' "

refreshing sleep—so well ventilated. It would make a splendid place for writing—undisturbed and airy. But unfortunately I have matters to attend to and must leave right away. Good day to you."

"Good day, Sir," said the sergeant. "You'll find the exit at the end of the passage."

At the front door of the police station the Doctor paused.

"My goodness!" he muttered. "I haven't any money to pay the coach back to Ashby. I wonder if Sir William would lend me a guinea."

And he turned back. But at the superintendent's office he was told that the Justice of Peace had gone off hunting for the day and wouldn't be back till tomorrow morning.

Once more he set out to leave the station. But at the door he paused again.

"I might as well take the rest of my loaf with me," he murmured. "It belongs to me after all—and I'll need it if I'm to get to Ashby without a penny in my pockets."

And he hurried back to his cell.

He found a policeman putting the place in order.

"Excuse me," said the Doctor. "Don't let me disturb your sweeping. I just came back for something I left behind me. Ah, there it is—my loaf! Thank you. Excellent bread you have here."

And after inquiring at the superintendent's office on the way out for the name of the baker who supplied the police station, John Dolittle sallied forth to freedom with half a loaf under his arm.

· The Fourth Chapter ·

NIGHTSHADE THE VIXEN

PENNILESS, but happy, the Doctor walked through the seaport town till he reached the marketplace in the center. At this point three big highways met: one from the north, one from the south and one from the east.

After admiring the town hall—it was a very beautiful and ancient building—the Doctor was about to set off along the road to the eastward. But he had not gone more than a pace or two before he paused, thinking. It occurred to him that it would be wiser if he found some other way to return to Ashby than that by which he had come.

He, therefore, changed his direction and swung off along the road to the south, intending to work his way back around to Ashby by some route where he would run no risk of meeting the people who had seen him in the coach or the Shottlake inn.

It was a pleasant morning. The sun was shining, sparrows chirping; and he felt, as he strutted down the road with his loaf of bread under his arm, that in such weather it was a pleasure to be alive.

Before long he had left the last houses of the town behind and found himself in the open country. About noon he came to a crossroads where a signpost, pointing down a very pretty little country lane, read **TO APPLEDYKE**, TEN MILES.

That looks a nice road, said the Doctor to himself. And it runs in the right direction for me. I like the sound of Appledyke too.

So, although he was not very far yet from the seaport town which he had left, he struck off eastward along the country lane to Appledyke.

Soon he decided it was lunchtime and looked about him for a brook where he might get a drink of clean water to wash down his dry-bread meal. Over to his right he saw a place where the land dipped downward into a hollow filled with trees and bushes.

"I'll bet there's a brook down there," the Doctor murmured. "It is certainly most delightful country, this."

Then he climbed over a stile and set off across the meadows, that led down into the hollow.

He found his brook, all right; and the banks of it, shaded by the trees, formed the most charming picnicking ground anyone could wish for. After he had taken a drink the Doctor with a grateful sigh sank down on the grass at the foot of a spreading oak, took out his loaf, and began to eat.

Presently he saw a starling hopping around near him, and he threw him some crumbs. While the bird was eating them the Doctor noticed that one of his wings seemed queer, and on examining it he found that the feathers were all stuck together with tar. The tar had hardened and the wing would not spread open the way it should. John Dolittle soon put it right and the bird flew off about his business. After his lunch the Doctor felt that before going on with his journey he would like to rest awhile in this pleasant spot. So he

"He came to a crossroads"

leaned back against the trunk of the oak tree and soon he fell asleep to the music of the murmuring brook.

When he awoke he found four foxes, a vixen with three cubs, sitting patiently beside him waiting till he should finish his nap.

"Good afternoon," said the vixen. "My name is Nightshade. Of course, I've heard a lot about you. But I had no idea you were in the district. I've often thought of coming all the way to Puddleby to see you. I'm awfully glad I didn't miss you on this visit. A starling told me you were here."

"Well," said the Doctor, sitting up, "I'm glad to see you. What can I do for you?"

"One of these children of mine"—the vixen pointed toward her three round little cubs who were gazing at the famous Doctor in great awe—"one of these children has something wrong with his front paws. I wish you would take a look at him."

"Certainly," said the Doctor. "Come here, young fellow."

"He has never been able to run properly," said the mother as John Dolittle took the cub on his lap and examined him. "It has nearly cost us all our lives, his slow pace, when the dogs have been after us. The others can run beautifully. Can you tell me what's the matter with him?"

"Why, of course," said the Doctor, who now had the cub upside down on his knees with its four big paws waving in the air. "It's a case of flat feet. That's all. The muscles of the pads are weak. He can get no grip of the ground without good pad muscles. You'll have to exercise him morning and night. Make him rise on his toes like this: One, two! One, two! One, two!"

And the Doctor stood up and gave a demonstration of the exercise which in a person strengthens the arches of the feet and in a fox develops the muscles of the paw pads.

"If you make him do that twenty or thirty times every morning and every night I think you'll soon find his speed will get better," said the Doctor.

"Thank you very much," said the vixen. "I have the greatest difficulty making my children do anything regularly. Now you hear what the Doctor says, Dandelion: every morning and every night, thirty times, up on your toes as high as you can go. I don't want any flat-footed cubs in my family. We've always been—great heavens! Listen!"

The mother fox had stopped speaking, the beautiful brush

of her tail straight and quivering, her nose outstretched, pitiful terror staring from her wide-open eyes. And in the little silence that followed, from over the rising ground away off to the northeastward, came the dread sound that makes every fox's heart stand still.

"*The horn!*" she whispered through chattering teeth. "They're out! It's th—th—the huntsman's horn!"

As he looked at the trembling creature John Dolittle was reminded of the occasion that had made him an enemy of fox hunting for life—when he had met an old dog fox one evening lying half dead with exhaustion under a tangle of blackberries.

As the horn rang out again the poor vixen began running round her cubs like a crazy thing.

"Oh, what *shall* I do?" she moaned. "The children! If it wasn't for them I could perhaps give the dogs the slip. Oh, why did I bring them out in daylight to see you? I suppose I was afraid you might be gone if I waited till after dark. Now I've left our scent behind us, all the way from Broad Meadows, as plain as the nose on your face. And I've come right into the wind. What a fool I was! What shall I do? What shall I do?"

As the horn sounded the third time, louder and nearer, joined by the yelping of hounds in full cry, the little cubs scuttled to their mother and cowered under her.

A very firm look came into the Doctor's face.

"What pack is this?" he asked. "Do you know the name of it?"

"It's probably the Ditcham—their kennels are just the other side of Hallam's Acre. It might be the Wiltborough, over from Buckley Downs—they sometimes hunt this way. But mostly likely it's the Ditcham—the best pack in these parts. They were after me last week. But my sister crossed

" 'It's a case of flat feet' "

my trail just below Fenton Ridge and they went after her—
and got her. There's the horn again! Oh, what a fool I was to
bring these children out in daylight!"

"Don't worry, Nightshade," said the Doctor. "Even if it's
the Ditcham and the Wiltborough together, they're not going to get you today—nor your children, either. Let the cubs
get into my pockets—come on, hop in, young fellows—so.
Now you, Nightshade, come inside the breast of my coat.
That's the way—get further around toward the back. And
you can stick your feet and your brush into the tail-pocket.

And when I've buttoned it up like this—see?—you will be completely covered. Can you breathe all right back there?"

"Yes, I can breathe," said the vixen. "But it won't do us much good to be out of sight. The hounds can smell us—that's the way they run us down—with their noses."

"Yes, I know," said the Doctor. "But the men can't smell you. I can deal with the dogs all right. But you mustn't be seen by the men. Keep as still as a stone, all four of you—don't move or try to run for it, whatever happens."

And then John Dolittle, with his coat bulging with foxes in all directions, stood in a little clearing in the wooded hollow and awaited the oncoming of the Ditcham Hunt in full cry.

The mingled noises of the dogs, men, horns, and horses grew louder. And soon, peeping through the crossing branches of his cover, the Doctor saw the first hounds come in view at the top of the ridge. For a moment the leaders paused and sniffed the wind. Then in a beeline for the bottom of the hollow they came on down, stretched at full speed. Over the ridge and after them came the rest of the pack; and close behind the dogs rode the men in red coats on fine, swift horses.

Ahead of most of the huntsmen galloped one man, old, lean, and white-haired—Sir William Peabody, the Master of the Foxhounds. Halfway down the slope he turned in his saddle and called to a man on a gray mare close behind him.

"Jones, they're making for the spinney. Don't let the leaders break into it before we've got it surrounded. Watch Galloway; he's rods ahead. Mind, he doesn't put the fox out the other side—Watch Galloway!"

Then the man on the gray mare spurted ahead, cracking a long whip and calling, "Galloway! Here, Galloway!"

As the Doctor peered through the foliage he saw that the

leading hound was now quite close. But, wonderfully trained to the huntsmen's command, Galloway suddenly slackened his pace within a few yards of the trees and remained, yelping and barking, for the others to come up.

Over the ridge more riders came pouring—fat parsons on stocky cobs, country squires on hacks, ladies on elegant, dainty thoroughbreds—all the gentry of the neighborhood.

"My goodness!" murmured the Doctor. "Was there ever anything so childish? All this fuss for a poor little fox!"

As the hounds, under the guidance of the men with long whips, spread, yelping, around all sides of the spinney, the people called and shouted to one another and the noise was tremendous.

"We'll get him," bellowed a fat farmer on a pony. "Hounds have gone all around now and scent don't go on. It's a killing, sure. Wait till Jones lets 'em into the spinney. We'll get him!"

"Oh, no, you won't," the Doctor muttered, the firm look coming back into his face. "Not today, my fat friend—not today."

The dogs, impatient and eager, sniffed and ran hither and thither, waiting for permission to enter the little patch of woods and finish the hunt.

Suddenly a command was given and instantly they leapt into the underbrush from all sides.

John Dolittle was standing in his clearing, with his hands over his pockets, trying to look all ways at once at the moment when the hounds broke in. But he had not known from which direction the vixen had entered and left her scent behind. And suddenly, before he knew it, four heavy dogs had leapt on his back, and he went down on the ground, simply smothered under a tangled pile of yelping, fighting foxhounds.

Kicking and punching in all directions, the Doctor struggled to his feet.

"Get away!" he said in dog language. "Lead the hunt somewhere else. This fox is mine."

The hounds, spoken to in their own tongue, now had no doubt as to who the little man was that they had knocked down.

"I'm awfully sorry, Doctor," said Galloway, a fine, deep-chested dog with a tan patch over one eye. "We had no idea it was you. We jumped on you from behind, you know. Why didn't you call to us while we were outside?"

"How could I?" said the Doctor irritably, pushing away a dog who was sniffing at his pocket. "How could I—with you duffers making all that din? Look out, here come the huntsmen. Don't let them see you smelling around me. Get the pack out of here, Galloway, quick."

"All right, Doctor. But it smells to me as though you had more than one fox in your pockets," said Galloway.

"I've got a whole family," said the Doctor. "And I mean to keep them, too."

"Can't you let us have even one of them, Doctor?" asked the hound. "They're sneaky little things. They eat rabbits and chickens, you know."

"No," said the Doctor, "I can't. They have to get food for themselves. You have food given you. Go away—and hurry about it."

At that moment Sir William Peabody came up.

"Great heavens! Dolittle!" he exclaimed. "Haven't you left these parts yet? Did you see the fox? Hounds headed right down into this hollow."

"I wouldn't tell you, Will, if I had seen him," said the Doctor. "You know what I think of fox hunting."

"Sir William turned and drew rein"

"Funny thing!" muttered Sir William as he watched the dogs lurching about among the brush uncertainly. "They can't have lost the scent, surely. They came down here as firm as you like. Curious! . . . oh, heavens! I know what it is: They've followed your rotten fish smell—the seal! Good Lord!"

At that moment a cry came from the huntsmen that the hounds had found another scent and were going off to the southward. Sir William, who had dismounted, ran for his horse.

"Hang you, Dolittle!" he shouted. "You've led the hounds astray. I should have kept you in jail."

The few dogs remaining within the spinney were now melting away like shadows. One of the fox cubs stirred in the Doctor's pocket. Sir William had already mounted his horse outside.

"Goodness, I forgot again!" muttered the Doctor. "I must get that guinea . . . I say, Will!"

Then John Dolittle, his pockets full of foxes, ran out of the spinney after the Master of the Hunt.

"Listen, Will!" he called. "Would you lend me a guinea? I haven't any money to get to Ashby with."

Sir William turned in his saddle and drew rein.

"I'll lend you five guineas—or ten—John," said the magistrate, "if you'll only get out of this district and stop putting my hounds on false scents. Here you are."

"Thanks, Will," said the Doctor, taking the money and dropping it in his pocket on top of one of the cubs. "I'll send it back to you by mail."

Then he stood there by the edge of the spinney and watched the huntsmen, hallooing and galloping, disappear over the skyline to the southward.

"What a childish sport!" he murmured. "I can't understand what they see in it. Really, I can't. Grown men rushing about the landscape on horseback, caterwauling and blowing tin horns—all after one poor little wild animal! Perfectly childish!"

Returning to the side of the brook within the shelter of the trees, the Doctor took the foxes out of his pocket and set them on the ground.

"Well," said the vixen, "I had often heard that you were a

great man, John Dolittle, but I never realized till now what a truly marvelous person you were. I don't know how to thank you. I'm all overcome—Dandelion, get away from that water!"

PART IV

· The First Chapter ·

BACK TO THE CIRCUS

AND now, with money in his pocket to pay for a ride, John Dolittle set about finding a coach that would carry him back in the direction of Ashby.

At the village of Appledyke his little country lane led him onto a bigger highway running north and south. Making inquiries of the village blacksmith, he found that coaches plied this road and that he could expect one to pass in about half an hour. So, after buying some toffee at the one small shop which Appledyke could boast of, the Doctor settled down to wait, munching sweetmeats to pass the time.

About four o'clock in the afternoon a coach came along and took him to the next large town. From there he caught a night coach going east; and in the early hours of the following morning he was back within ten miles of Ashby again.

The remainder of the journey he thought he had better do on foot for safety's sake. So after he had a shave and a breakfast and a rest at an inn, he set out to walk the short remaining distance.

The way the Doctor first knew that he was nearing the circus was by hearing Jip's bark in the distance. The sound was joined by two other barks. And presently, rounding a bend in the highway, he found Jip, Toby, and Swizzle all yapping about the foot of a tree, up which they had chased a black cat. Still farther down the road he saw the tail end of the wagon train winding on its way.

As soon as he came in view the dogs forgot all about the cat and came racing down the road.

"Doctor! Doctor!" yelped Jip. "How did everything go off? Did Sophie get away?"

Then the three of them jumped all over him, and he had to answer a hundred questions at once. From beginning to end he told the story of his adventurous journey to the sea. And when a little later he overtook the circus train and reached his own wagon he had to tell it all over again for the benefit of the rest of his delighted family.

Dab-Dab hustled around and prepared a meal right away —a sort of tea-and-supper-combined arrangement; and she kept the rest of the household busy pulling out the bed linen to be aired, so that the Doctor should have dry sheets to sleep in.

Then Matthew Mugg got wind of his great friend's arrival, and he came and joined the party, and the story had to be told a third time.

"It was a great piece of work, Doctor," said he, "couldn't have gone better. Blossom never got the least suspicious that you was in it at all."

"What's happened to Higgins?" asked the Doctor.

"Oh, 'e's doing honest work now. Took a stableman's job in Ashby. Good thing, too! 'E's no loss to the circus business anyhow."

"Has Blossom put on any extra act to take Sophie's place?" asked the Doctor.

"No," said Matthew. "We were short'anded for a bit. But

"All yapping about the foot of an oak tree"

Hercules the strong man is back on the job now and the show's as good as ever."

"And we've made lots of money with our part of it, Doctor," cried Too-Too. "How much do you think the pushmi-pullyu took in last week?"

"I've no idea."

"Twelve pounds, nine shillings, and sixpence!"

"Great heavens!" cried the Doctor. "That's enormous—twelve pounds a week! That's more than I ever made in the best days of my practice. Why, we'll soon be able to retire at that rate!"

"What do you mean, retire, Doctor?" asked Toby, pushing his head up onto the Doctor's knee.

"Well, we hadn't meant to stay in the business for good, you know," said John Dolittle. "I have work of my own to look after in Puddleby . . . and . . . and . . . oh, heaps of things to attend to."

"I see," said Toby sadly. "I thought you were going to stay with us for quite a while."

"But how about the Dolittle Circus, Doctor?" asked Swizzle. "Aren't you going to try that idea—the reformed show we talked about?"

"It's a great notion, Doctor," Jip put in. "All the animals are crazy about the scheme. They've been working out the details of their own part of the performance."

"And what about our theater, Doctor—the Animals' Own Theater?" Gub-Gub put in. "I've written a play for it since you've been gone. It's called *The Bad Tomato*. I do the comic fat-lady's part. I know my lines by heart already."

"And what about the house in Puddleby? That's what I'd like to know?" said Dab-Dab, angrily brushing the crumbs off the table. "All you animals ever think of is having a good time. You never think of the Doctor and what he wants. You never think of the house going to ruin back there and the garden turning into a jungle. The Doctor has his own work and his own home and his own life to attend to."

A little silence followed the housekeeper's furious outburst, and Toby and Swizzle rather shamefacedly retired under the table.

"Well," said the Doctor at last, "there is something in what Dab-Dab says. I do think as soon as the pushmi-pullyu has made enough to pay back the sailor for his boat—and a little to spare—we ought to think about leaving the business."

"Oh, dear!" sighed Toby. "The Dolittle Circus would have been such a wonderful show!"

"Heigh-ho!" said Gub-Gub. "And I would have been simply splendid as a fat lady. I always thought I ought to have been a comic actor."

"Huh!" snorted Dab-Dab. "Last week you said you ought to have been a greengrocer."

"Well," said Gub-Gub. "I could be both—a comic green-grocer. Why not?"

That same night Blossom's circus entered the town of Stowbury. And, as usual, before dawn the next morning the tents had been set up and everything gotten in readiness for showing.

As soon as the news of the Doctor's arrival got about, Mr. Blossom came to see him. And from all appearances John Dolittle decided that no suspicions had been aroused in the mind of the ringmaster by his "business" trip.

Another caller at the Doctor's stand that morning was Hercules the strong man. Hercules had never forgotten the kind attention shown him at the time of his accident, and he was glad to find that his friend had returned. His pleasant chat was cut short, however, when he suddenly discovered that it was time for him to give his first performance. The Doctor accompanied him back to his stand.

While returning across the circus enclosure the Doctor noticed, as he passed the tent of Fatima the snake charmer, a strong odor of chloroform. Fearing an accident might have happened, he went inside and found that Fatima was out at the moment. Within the tent the smell was stronger, and it seemed to be coming from the snake box. The Doctor looked into the box and found the six snakes in a almost

" 'They hated it,' the snake said"

unconscious state from the drug. One of them still had sense
enough left to tell the Doctor, in answer to his questions,
that Fatima always dosed them with chloroform on hot
days, when they were too lively, in order to make them easier to handle for her performance. They hated it, the snake
said, because it gave them headaches.

On this pleasant, sunny morning the Doctor had forgotten, for a moment, the wretched condition of many of the
animals, which had so often sickened him of the whole circus business. This piece of senseless cruelty threw him into

a boiling rage, and he hurried off at once to look for Blossom.

He found him in the big tent and Fatima with him. The Doctor firmly demanded that the custom of chloroforming the snakes be forbidden. Blossom merely smiled and pretended to be busy with other matters, while Fatima hurled a lot of vulgar language at the Doctor's head.

Discouraged and sad, John Dolittle left the tent, intending to return to his own wagon. The gates were now open and the crowds were coming in thick and fast. The Doctor was wondering how American blacksnakes would manage in the English climate if he contrived their escape, when he noticed a throng of visitors collecting about a platform down at the other end of the enclosure.

At this moment Matthew came up and joined him, and together they started toward the platform. On this the Doctor now saw a man who advertised himself as Dr. Brown, delivering a lecture about the wonders of his pills and ointments, which could cure, in one dose, all the ailments known to mankind.

"What arrangement has this fellow with Blossom?" the Doctor asked of Matthew.

"Oh, he pays him a rake-off," said the cat's-meat man. "Blossom gets so much on all he takes in. He's going on with us to the next three towns, I hear. Doing a good trade too, ain't he?"

Indeed, Dr. Brown was very busy. Country yokels, after listening to his noisy medical lectures, were buying his wares right and left.

"Go and get me a pot of that ointment, will you, Matthew?" said the Doctor. "Here's some money—and get me a box of the pills as well."

"All right," said Matthew with a grin. "But I don't reckon you'll find them much good."

The cat's-meat man returned with the purchases and the Doctor took them to his wagon. There he opened them, smelled them, examined them and tested them with chemicals from his little black bag.

"Rubbish and bunkum!" he cried when he had ended. "This is just highway robbery. Why did I ever go into this rotten show business? Matthew, get me a stepladder."

The cat's-meat man went out, disappeared behind some tents, and presently returned with the stepladder.

"Thank you," said the Doctor, putting it on his shoulder and marching off toward the platform. There was a dangerous light in his eyes.

"What are you going to do, Doctor?" asked Matthew, hurrying after him.

"I'm going to give a medical lecture myself," said the Doctor. "Those people are not going to pay their money for quack rubbish if I can help it."

Jip, who was sitting at the door of his wagon, suddenly pricked up his ears and sprang to his feet.

"Toby," he called over his shoulder, "the Doctor's going over to the patent-medicine man's platform. He's got a stepladder. He looks awfully mad about something. There's going to be a row, I fancy. Get Swizzle and let's go and see the fun."

John Dolittle, on reaching the crowd at Brown's lecture stand, set up his stepladder right opposite the speaker, and Matthew Mugg cleared a space around it so the audience shouldn't knock it over while the Doctor climbed it.

At the moment of his arrival, Brown was holding up in his left hand a pot of ointment.

"This preparation which I 'old in my 'and, ladies and gentlemen," he bawled, "is the greatest remedy in the world for sciatica, lumbago, neuralgia, ague, and gout. It 'as been hendorsed by all the leadin' physicians. It is the same what is used by the royal family of Belgium and the Shah of Persia. One application of this marvelous remedy will—"

At this point another voice, still more powerful, interrupted the lecture. The people all turned around, and there behind them, perched on a stepladder stood a little round man with a battered high hat on his head.

"Ladies and gentleman," said the Doctor, "what this man is telling you is not true. His ointment contains nothing but lard mixed with a little perfume. His pills are no good either. I do not recommend you to buy any."

For a moment there was a dead silence. While Dr. Brown was trying to think up something to say, the voice of a woman, Fatima the snake charmer, was heard from the edge of the crowd.

"Don't you listen to him," she yelled, pointing a fat finger at John Dolittle. "He's nothing but a showman. He doesn't know anything about medicines. Push 'im orf 'is ladder."

"Just a minute," said the Doctor, addressing the crowd again. "It is true that I am in the show business—for the moment. But I am a medical graduate of the University of Durham. I am prepared to stand by what I have said. These preparations that this man is trying to sell you are worthless. Also I have grave doubts about his education in dentistry, and I do not advise any of you to have your teeth touched by him."

The crowd now began to get restless. Several people had already purchased Brown's wares and these could now be seen making their way to the platform and demanding their money back. Brown refused it and tried to make another address to his audience in answer to the Doctor's statements.

"Listen," yelled John Dolittle from his ladder, "I challenge this man to produce a medical degree or credentials of any kind to prove that he is a qualified doctor or dentist. He is a quack."

"You're a fake yourself," yelled Brown. "I'll have the law on you for libel."

"Push 'im down!" howled Fatima. "Mob 'im!"

But the people did not seem inclined to follow her orders. Presently the Doctor was recognized by one of his old patients among the audience—just as he had been in the case of the strong man's accident some weeks before. A little old lady suddenly waved an umbrella above the crowd.

"That's John Dolittle," she shouted, "who cured my son Joe of whooping cough back in Puddleby ten years ago. Like to die he was. He's a real doctor—none better in the West Country. T'other's a quack. Ye be fools if ye turn a deaf ear to what John Dolittle tells ye."

Then other voices were heard here and there among the crowd. The general restlessness increased. More people struggled forward to Brown's platform to bring back the wares they had bought. A growing murmur arose.

"Mob 'im! Knock 'im down!" yelled Fatima, trying to make herself heard.

Dr. Brown thrust aside two men who had climbed up onto his stand for their money, came to the edge of the platform, and opened his mouth to begin another medical lecture.

But a large, well-aimed turnip suddenly sailed across the heads of the audience and hit him squarely in the face. The mobbing had begun—but it wasn't directed against John

Dolittle. Soon carrots, potatoes, stones, all manner of missiles, were flying through the air.

"Grab 'im!" yelled the crowd. "He's a crook."

And the next moment the whole audience surged toward the platform yelling and shaking their fists.

· The Second Chapter ·

THE PATENT-MEDICINE RIOTS

JOHN DOLITTLE himself grew a little alarmed as he saw what an ugly mood the crowd was now beginning to show. When he had first mounted his ladder and interrupted the quack doctor's lecture he had meant to do no more than warn the people against buying fake medicines. But as he watched the throng swarm over the platform, wrecking and smashing it on the way, he began to fear for Brown's safety.

When the riot was at its height the police arrived. Even they had considerable difficulty in calming the crowd. They had to use their clubs to make them listen at all. There were many broken heads and bloody noses. Finally the police saw that their only chance of restoring order would be to clear the circus enclosure altogether.

This was done—in spite of the people's objection that they had only just come in and wanted their admission money back before they left. Then the circus was ordered by the police to remain closed until further instructions.

It was not long before the further instructions were forthcoming. Much indignation had been aroused throughout the respectable town of Stowbury over the whole affair. And the mayor sent word to Blossom about noon that he and the aldermen would be obliged to him if he would pack up his circus and take it out of their town immediately.

Brown had escaped and got away across country long before this. But that wasn't the end of the affair so far as John Dolittle was concerned. Blossom, already annoyed, became so furious when the mayor's order was brought that everybody thought he was going to have a fit. Fatima had been railing against the Doctor to him all the morning; and on hearing the last bit of news, which meant considerable loss, he got almost black in the face.

Many of the showmen were with him when the policeman delivered the order. On them too Fatima had been working, trying to arouse bad feeling against the Doctor.

"Blast it!" yelled Blossom, rising to his feet and reaching for a thick walking stick that stood behind his wagon door. "I'll teach him to get my circus closed up! Come on, some of you fellows!"

With waving fists Fatima and four or five of the showmen standing near followed the ringmaster as he marched off toward the Doctor's stand.

Both Jip and Matthew had also been hanging around Blossom's wagon. They too now departed, Jip running ahead to warn the Doctor and the cat's-meat man going off in a wholly different direction.

On their way to the Doctor's wagon Blossom and his party of vengeance were joined by several tent riggers and others. By the time they arrived at his door they numbered a good dozen. To their surprise the Doctor came out to meet them.

"Good afternoon," said John Dolittle politely. "What can I do for you?"

Blossom tried to speak, but his anger was too much for him—nothing more than spluttering gurgles came from his throat.

"You've done enough for us already," shouted one of the men.

"We're going to do for you now," screamed Fatima.

"You've got the show turned out of the town," growled a third, "one of the best places on the road. You've cost us a week's pay."

"You've been doing your best to put my show on the blink," snarled Blossom, finding his voice at last, "ever since you've been with us. But, by jiminy, you've gone too far this time!"

Without further words the group of angry men, led by the ringmaster, rushed upon the Doctor and he went down under a football scrum of kicking feet and punching fists.

Poor Jip did his best to drag them off. But it was little help he could give against twelve such enemies. He couldn't see the Doctor at all. He was beginning to wonder where Matthew was when he saw the cat's-meat man running toward the fight from the other side of the enclosure. And beside him ran an enormous man in pink tights.

On reaching the scrum the big man began pulling off the showmen by their feet or hair and tossing them aside as though they were wisps of straw.

Finally Hercules the strong man—for it was he—had thinned the fight down to two, Blossom and the Doctor. These still rolled upon the ground trying to throttle one another. With a hand the size of a leg of mutton, Hercules grasped the ringmaster by the neck and shook him like a rat.

" 'I'll slap your face' "

"If you don't be'ave yourself, Alexander," he said quietly, "I'll slap your face and knock your brains out."

There was a little silence while the rest of the showmen picked themselves up from the grass

"Now," said Hercules, still grasping Blossom by the collar, "what's this all about? What are you all settin' on the Doc for? Ought to be ashamed—a good dozen of yer—and him the littlest of all!"

"He went and told the people that Brown's ointment wasn't no good," said Fatima. "Got 'em all worked up, asking for their money back. Called him a fake in front of the audience—and 'im the biggest fake that ever walked himself."

"You're a nice one to talk about fakes!" said Hercules. "Didn't I see you painting bands on your pore harmless snakes last week—to make 'em look like real deadly ones? This man's a good doctor. He couldn't 'ave mended my busted ribs for me if he wasn't."

"He's got the show turned out of the town," growled one of the men. "We had our thirty-mile trip from Ashby for nothing—and another forty-mile one ahead of us before we take in a penny. That's what your precious *doctor* has done for you!"

"He's not going any farther with my show," spluttered Blossom. "I've taken about all I'm going to stand from him."

He wriggled himself out of the strong man's grasp and advancing toward the Doctor shook a finger in his face.

"You're fired," he yelled. "Understand? You leave my show today—now."

"Very well," said the Doctor quietly. And he turned away toward the door of his wagon.

"Just a minute," Hercules called after him. "Do you want to go, Doctor?"

John Dolittle paused and turned back.

"Well, Hercules," he said doubtfully, "it's rather hard to answer that question."

"What he *wants* 'as got nothing to do with it," said Fatima. "The boss 'as fired 'im. That settles it. 'E's got to go."

As the Doctor looked into the jeering eyes of this woman who hated him, he thought of the snakes who were in her care. Then he thought of several other circus animals whose condition he had hoped to improve—of Beppo, the old wagon horse who should have been pensioned off years ago.

And while he hesitated Swizzle pushed his damp nose up into his hand and Toby plucked at the tail of his coat.

"No, Hercules," he said at last. "All things considered, I do not want to go. But if I'm sent away there's nothing I can do about it, is there?"

"No," said the strong man. "But there's something others can do about it. Look here"—he spun Blossom around by the shoulder and shook an enormous fist under his nose. "This man's an honest man. Brown was a crook. If the Doctor goes, I go too. And if I go, my nephews, the trapeze acrobats, will come with me. And I've a notion that Hop the clown will join us. Now how about it?"

Mr. Alexander Blossom, proprietor of the greatest show on earth, hesitated, chewing his mustache in dismay and perplexity. With Sophie the seal gone, deserted by the strong man, the trapeze brothers, his best clown, and the pushmi-pullyu, his circus would be sadly reduced. While he pondered, Fatima's face was a study. If looks could have killed, both Hercules and the Doctor would have died that day twice over.

"Well," said the ringmaster at last in quite a different voice, "let's talk this over friendly like. There's no need for hard feelings—and no sense in breaking up the show just because we've come a cropper in one town."

"If I stay," said the Doctor, "I insist that no more fake medicines be sold while I am with you."

"Huh!" snorted Fatima. "See what he's goin' to do? 'E's beginnin' again. 'E's goin' to tell you how to run your show."

"Also," said the Doctor, "I shall require that this woman no longer have the handling of snakes or any other animals. If you want to keep me, she must go. I will buy her snakes from her myself."

" 'He's bought six fat snakes with it!' "

Well, in spite of Fatima's screaming indignation, matters were at last arranged peaceably. But that night, when Too-Too was sitting on the steps of the wagon listening to a brother owl who was hooting to him from the town ceme-tery, Dab-Dab came out and joined him, with tears in her eyes.

"I don't know what we'll ever do with the Doctor," she said wearily. "Really I don't. He has taken every penny we had in the money box—the whole twelve pounds, nine shil-lings, and sixpence that we had saved up to go back to Pud-dleby with. And what do you think he has gone and spent it on? He's bought six fat snakes with it!" (Dab-Dab burst into a renewed flood of tears.) "And he . . . he . . . has put them in my flour bin to keep till . . . till he can get a proper bed for them!"

· The Third Chapter ·

NINO

AFTER the departure of Fatima the snake charmer, John Dolittle liked the life of the circus a good deal better. It had mostly been the thought that he was not doing anything to help the animals that had made him so often speak against it. But now that he had sent Sophie back to her husband, freed the snakes from a life of slavery and chloroform, and forbidden the selling of quack medicines, he began to feel that his presence here was doing good.

And then Blossom, ever since the medical lecture riot, had shown him a great deal more respect. The ringmaster had always known that he had a good thing in the pushmi-pullyu. And if it had not been for his blind rage at being turned out of the town by the mayor, and for Fatima's eternal nagging against the Doctor, he would never have dreamed of trying to get rid of him at all.

John Dolittle's own popularity with the circus people themselves was in the end improved greatly by the incident at Stowbury. In spite of the fact that she had successfully turned many of the showmen against the Doctor, Fatima herself had always been disliked by almost everyone. And

"They had made their usual procession
through the streets"

when it became known that the Doctor had brought about
her departure he was very soon forgiven for the loss caused
by the circus being ordered out of the town.

However, his real power and influence with the show people did not properly begin until the day that the talking
horse fell sick.

The circus had moved on to a town called Bridgeton, a
large manufacturing center, where good business was expected by Blossom. The animals and clowns and bareback
riders and the rest had made their usual procession through

the streets; big bills were posted all over the place. And when the enclosure was opened to the public, great throngs of people had crowded up to the gates. It looked like one of the best weeks the circus had ever known.

At two o'clock the show at the big tent was to begin. Outside the entrance a large sign was set up showing the program: Mademoiselle Firefly, the Bareback Rider; the Pinto Brothers, Daring Trapeze Artists; Hercules, the Strongest Man on Earth; Hop, the Side-Splitting Clown, and His Comedy Wonder-Dog, Swizzle; Jojo, the Dancing Elephant, and (in large letters) NINO, the World-Famous Talking Horse.

Now this Nino was just an ordinary, cream-colored cob who had been trained to answer signals. Blossom had bought him from a Frenchman; and with him he had bought the secret of his so-called talking. In his act he didn't talk at all really. All he did was to stamp his hoof or wag his head a certain number of times to give answers to the questions Blossom asked him in the ring.

"How many do three and four make, Nino?" Blossom would say. Then Nino would stamp the floor seven times. And if the answer was yes, he would nod his head up and down, and if it was no, he would shake it from side to side. Of course, he didn't know what was being asked of him at all, as a matter of fact. And the way he knew what answers to give was from the signals that Blossom made to him secretly. When he wanted Nino to say yes, the ringmaster would scratch his left ear; when he wanted him to answer no, he would fold his arms, and so on. The secret of all these signals Blossom kept jealously to himself. But, of course, the Doctor knew all about them because Nino had told him how the whole performance was carried on.

Now, in advertising the circus Blossom always put Nino, the World-Famous Talking Horse, before all the other acts in importance. It was a popular performance and the children loved shouting questions down to the little plump cob and seeing him answer with his feet or his head.

Well, on the circus's first day in Bridgeton, a little before the show in the big tent was to begin, the Doctor and the ringmaster were in the clown's dressing room talking. Suddenly in rushed the head stableman in a great state of excitement.

"Mr. Blossom," he cried, "Nino's sick! Layin' in his stall with 'is eyes closed. The show's due to begin in fifteen minutes and I can't do nothing with 'im—can't even get 'im on his feet."

With a hearty curse Blossom rushed out and tore away in the direction of the stables, while the Doctor followed him on the run.

When they got to Nino's stall Blossom and the Doctor found the horse in a bad state. His breathing was fast and heavy. With difficulty he was made to stand up on his feet, but for walking even a few steps he seemed far too shaky and weak.

"Darn the luck!" muttered the manager. "If he can't perform it will queer the whole week's showing. We've posted him as the star act. The crowd will want to know about it if they don't see him."

"You'll have to make a speech and explain," said the Doctor. "That horse has a bad fever. I doubt if he can leave his stall today."

"Good heavens, man, he'll have to!" cried Blossom. "We'll likely have the audience asking for its money back if he don't appear. We can't have any more riots like—"

At that moment a boy came up.

"Five minutes to two, Mr. Blossom. Pierce wants to know if you are all ready."

"Hang it!" said the manager. "I can't take the ring for the first act. I must get Nino fixed up before I can come on."

"We ain't got nobody else, sir," said the boy. "Robinson 'asn't got back yet."

"Lord, what a day!" groaned the manager. "Well, the show can't open without a ringmaster, that's sure. And I can't leave Nino yet. I don't know what—"

"Excuse me, governor," said a voice behind him. And turning, Blossom looked into the crossed eyes of Matthew Mugg.

"Couldn't I take your place, Boss?" said the cat's-meat man. "I know your whole line of talk by heart. I could introduce the acts—same as you—and nobody know the difference."

"Well," said Blossom looking him up and down, "you're about the scrubbiest ringmaster I ever see'd. But beggars can't be choosers. Come with me—quick—and I'll give you these clothes."

Then, while the Doctor turned his attention to Nino, Blossom and Matthew made off on the run for the dressing rooms. There, with the aid of Theodosia (who put a large swift pleat in Blossom's riding breeches) and a little rouge and a false mustache from the clown's makeup box, Mr. Mugg was transformed from a cat's-meat man into a ringmaster. The ambition of his life was realized at last. And as he swaggered into the ring and looked up at the sea of faces around him, his chest swelled with dignity, while Theodosia, watching him through a slit in the tent flap, glowed with wifely pride and prayed that the pleat in his riding breeches would hold till the show was over.

In the meantime from an examination of Nino the Doctor became certain that there was no hope of his recovering in time to perform that day. He went and got some large pills from his black bag and gave him two. Presently Blossom, now dressed in a jersey and flannel pants, joined him.

"You can't have this horse perform today, Mr. Blossom," said the Doctor, "nor for a week, probably, at least."

"Well," said the ringmaster, throwing up his hands in despair, "we're just ruined—that's all—ruined! That row up in Stowbury got into the papers, and now if we have another frost here, we're done for. And if Nino don't go on, the crowd's going to ask for their money back, sure as you're alive. He's the star act. We might manage if we had another act to put on in his place, but I haven't a blessed thing for an extra. And it was a short program anyhow. We're ruined. Darn it, I never saw such a run of rotten luck!"

Poor Blossom seemed genuinely crestfallen. While the Doctor looked at him thoughtfully, a horse in the stall next to Nino's neighed softly. It was Beppo, the veteran wagon horse. A smile came into the Doctor's face.

"Look here, Mr. Blossom," said he quietly, "I think I can help you out of this trouble, but if I do you've got to promise me a few things. I know a good deal more about animals than you suppose I do. I've given up the best part of my life to studying them. You advertised that Nino understood you and could answer any questions you put to him. You and I know that's not so, don't we? The trick was done by a system of signals. But it took the public in. Now I'm going to tell you a secret of my own, which I don't boast about because nobody would believe me if I did. I can talk to horses in their own language and understand them when they talk back to me."

Blossom was staring down moodily at the floor while the Doctor spoke. But at the last words he gazed up at John Dolittle frowning.

"Are you crazy?" he said, "or didn't I hear straight? Talk to

" 'You can't have this horse perform today' "

animals in their own language! Look 'ere, I've been in the
show business thirty-seven years, knocked around with animals ever since I was a nipper. And I know there ain't no
such thing as a man talking with a horse in horse language.
You got a cheek to tell me a yarn like that—me, Alexander
Blossom!"

· The Fourth Chapter ·

ANOTHER TALKING HORSE

I AM not telling you a yarn," said the Doctor quietly. "I am telling you the truth. But I can see that you will not believe me till I prove it to you."

"You bet I won't," sneered Blossom.

"Well, there are five horses in this stable, aren't there?" asked the Doctor. "And none of them can see me here where I stand, can they? Now if you will ask me to put some questions to any one of them I will endeavor to give you his answer."

"Oh, you're crazy!" said Blossom. "I ain't got time to fool with you."

"All right," said the Doctor. "My intention was to help, as I told you. But, of course, if you don't want my assistance, then that ends the matter."

He shrugged his shoulders and turned away. The noise of clapping sounded from the big tent.

"Ask Beppo," said Blossom, "what's the number of the stall he's in."

Beppo's was the second from the end. On his door was marked a large "2" in white paint.

197

"Do you wish to have him tell me the answer in horse language?" asked the Doctor, "or shall I have him tap the number?"

"Have him tap the partition with his foot, Professor," sneered Blossom. "I don't know no horse grammar; and I couldn't tell, t'other way, whether you was faking or not."

"Very good," said the Doctor. And from where he stood, quite invisible to Beppo, he made some snuffly breathing noises—rather as though he had a cold in his head. Immediately two taps sounded from stall No. 2.

Blossom's eyebrows went up in surprise. But almost immediately he shrugged his shoulders.

"Pshaw! Could easily 'ave been an accident. Maybe he just fell against the partition. Ask 'im—er—ask 'im 'ow many buttons I 'ave on my waistcoat—the one your cross-eyed assistant is wearing in the ring now."

"All right," said the Doctor. And he made some more snuffly noises, ending with a gentle whinny.

But this time, unintentionally, he did not include Beppo's name in his message. Now all the five horses in that stable knew Blossom's waistcoat very well, of course. And each one thought the question was being asked of him. Suddenly from every stall six sharp raps rang out, and even poor Nino lying in the straw with eyes closed, stretched and a hind leg and weakly kicked his door six times. Mr. Blossom's eyes looked as though they were going to pop out of his head.

"Now," said the Doctor smiling, "in case you should think that that was accidental too, I will ask Beppo to pull down the rag you see there hanging on his partition and to throw it up in the air."

In response to a few more words of horse language the rag, whose end hung over the top of the partition, suddenly disappeared. The Doctor had not moved. Blossom ran down the stable to look inside stall No. 2. There he found the aged wagon horse tossing the rag up in the air and catching it—rather like a school girl playing with a handkerchief.

"Now do you believe me?" asked the Doctor.

"Believe you!" cried Blossom. "I believe you're the man I want, all right. Come on down to the dressing room and let's put some togs on you."

"Just a minute," said the Doctor. "What do you mean to do?"

"Dress you up," said Blossom, "of course. You're going to do an act for us, ain't yer? Why you could take any cab horse and make a Nino of him. You said you was going to help me?"

"Yes," answered John Dolittle slowly, "and I will—after, as I told you, you have promised me a few things. I am willing to make Beppo provide your ring with a talking horse on certain conditions. Nino's act doesn't come on till the end of the show. We have a half hour to talk this over in."

"There's no need," cried Blossom, all excited. "I'll promise you any bloomin' thing. Why, if you can talk animals' language we'll make a fortune in a season! Lor' bless us! I never believed you could do it. You ought to 'ave joined the show business years ago. You'd 'ave bin a rich man by now—instead of a broken-down country doctor. Come on over and we'll pick you out some nifty togs. Can't go on in them baggy trousers; people 'ud think you'd never bin on a horse in your life."

Blossom and the Doctor left the stable and made their way across to the dressing rooms, where out of some of the well-traveled trunks the ringmaster began pulling costume after costume and piling them on the floor. While he was going through the gaudy clothes the Doctor laid down the conditions under which he would give the performance.

"Now, Mr. Blossom," said he, "ever since I have been with your concern I have noticed certain things that were distasteful to my ideas of honest business and the humanitarian treatment of animals. Some of these I have brought to your attention and in almost all cases you refused to listen to me."

"Why, Doctor," said Mr. Blossom, yanking a pair of red Persian trousers out of a trunk, "how can you say such a thing? Didn't I get rid of Brown and Fatima because you objected to 'em?"

"You parted with them because you had to," said the Doctor, "not to oblige me. I have felt very uneasy about being part of a show that I did not consider strictly honest. It would take a long time to go into all the details. For the present, the bargain I am going to strike with you is this: Beppo, the horse I will use for the talking act, is far too old to work. He has been in service now thirty-five years. I want him, as a reward for this help that he will give you, to be pensioned off for the remainder of his days, made comfortable, and given the kind of life he likes."

"I agree. Now how would this do?"

Blossom held up a cavalier's jerkin against the Doctor's chest. "No—too small. You ain't very high from the ground, but you're full-sized around the middle, all right."

"The other thing I want you to do," the Doctor went on, as Blossom turned back to the trunk for another costume, "is to put your menagerie in proper order. The cages are not cleaned often enough; some of the animals have not sufficient space for their needs. And many of them never get the kinds of food they like best."

"All right, Doc, we'll do anything in reason. I'll let you

" 'Why, Doctor, how can you say such a thing?' "

draw up a set of rules for the menagerie keeper and you can see that he toes the line. 'Ow would you like to be a western cowboy?"

"I wouldn't," said the Doctor. "They are inconsiderate to their cattle. And I don't approve of that silly business of flapping a hat in a horse's eyes to make him buck. Then, for the rest, I shall from time to time expect you to make many minor reforms for the animals' comfort. I shall expect you to treat my suggestions reasonably and cooperate with me for their welfare. What do you say?"

"I say it's a go, Doc," said Blossom. "We ain't begun yet. If you stay with my outfit for a year—with your gift of talking to animals—why!—I'll make every other circus look like a two-penny peepshow. Oh, my! 'Ere's the very thing—a cavalry uniform—Twenty-first Hussars. Just your size. Medals and all! Suits your complexion, too."

This time Blossom held a bright scarlet tunic over the Doctor's bosom and beamed on him with delight.

"Ever seen anything so nifty?" he chuckled. "My word! I tell yer—we'll make this town sit up! Could you get these things on your feet?"

"Oh, I daresay," said the Doctor, taking a gaudy pair of military riding boots from the ringmaster and sitting down to unlace his own. At that moment the door opened and a stableboy came in.

"Joe, you're just in time," said Blossom. "Run over to the stables and give Beppo a rubdown with the currycomb. He's going to do an act."

"Beppo!" cried the boy incredulously.

"That's what I said, block'ead!" shouted Blossom. "And put the green 'alter on 'im with the white rosettes—and braid 'is tail with a red ribbon. Hop about it!"

As the lad disappeared, the clown with Swizzle entered for a short rest between acts. The Doctor, in smart regimental breeches and top boots, was now buttoning up the scarlet tunic about his chin.

" 'Ow's my cross-eyed understudy doing?" asked Blossom.

"Governor, he's a wonder!!" said Hop, sinking into a chair. "A born ringmaster. You never heard such a voice. He's got a gift of gab, all right. Ready with a joke if anybody slips; cracking quips with the audience—I tell you, governor, you've got to look to your laurels if you leave him with the ladies for long. Who's the military gentleman? My hat, it's the Doctor! What's he going to do?"

At this moment another lad ran in.

"Only ten minutes before the last act goes on, Mr. Blossom," he cried.

"All right," said Blossom. "We can do it. Here's your sword belt, Doctor. How's the crowd, Frank?"

"Great!" said the boy. "Pleased as Punch! They brought the whole grammar school down at the last minute. And the Soldiers and Sailors Home is coming tonight. People standing two deep in the aisles. It's the biggest business we've played to this year."

· The Fifth Chapter ·

THE STAR GIVES
A GREAT PERFORMANCE

TREMENDOUS excitement now prevailed behind the scenes in Blossom's Mammoth Circus. As the clown, Hop, opened the dressing-room door to go back into the ring, mingled cheers and hand-clapping, the noise of a big audience's applause, reached the ears of John Dolittle and the manager.

"Listen, Hop," said Blossom, "pass the word to Mugg as you go back in that Nino is going to play anyway—in substitute—and the Doc here is doing the part of the trainer. Mugg can give 'em the introduction patter just the same. Tell 'im to lay it on thick. It's going to be the greatest little act we ever showed—better than Nino at his best."

"All right, governor," said the clown, grinning through his paint. "But I wish you had picked a better-looking horse."

At the last moment one of the Doctor's shoulder straps was found to be loose. Only two minutes now remained before his act was due. Someone flew off and found Theodosia and with frantic haste she put it right with a needle and thread. Then, complete in his gay and wonderful uniform, the Doctor ran out of the dressing room to join his partner,

" 'Listen, Hop!' "

Beppo, whose bridle was being held at the entrance to the big tent by the boy, Frank.

Poor Beppo did not look nearly as smart as the Doctor. Years of neglect and haphazard grooming could not be remedied by one currycombing. His coat was long and dingy-looking, his mane straggly and unkempt. In spite of the smart green and white headstall and the red ribbon in his plaited tail, he looked what he was: an old, old servant who had done his work faithfully for many, many years and gotten little credit or thanks for it.

"Oh, I say, Beppo!" the Doctor murmured in his ear as he

took the bridle from Frank. "Anyone would think you were going to a funeral. Brace up! Draw your head back, high. That's it. Now blow out your nostrils. . . . Ah, much better!"

"You know, Doctor," said Beppo, "you mightn't believe it, but I come of a very good family. My mother used to trace her pedigree way back to the battle charger that Julius Caesar used—the one he always rode when he reviewed the praetorian guard. My mother was very proud of it. She took first prizes, she did. But when the heavy battle chargers went out of fashion all the big military horses got put to draft work. That's how we came down in the world. Oughtn't we to rehearse this act a bit first? I've no idea of what I'm expected to do."

"No, we haven't time now," said John Dolittle. "We are liable to be called on any minute. But we'll manage. Just do everything I tell you—and put in any extras you think of yourself. Look out, you're drooping your head again. Remember your Roman ancestor. Chin up—that's the way. Arch your neck. Make your eyes flash. Look as though you were carrying an emperor who owned the earth. . . . Fine! That's the style! Now you look great."

Within the big canvas theater Mr. Matthew Mugg, ringmaster for a day, was still covering himself with glory, bossing the greatest show on earth with creditable skill and introducing the performers with much oratory and unusual grammar. He was having the time of his life and making the most of it.

In between the acts of the Pinto brothers and the strong man, he saw Hop return into the ring and recommence his antics, which always so delighted the children. As the clown did a somersault past the ringmaster's nose, Matthew heard him whisper, "The boss is putting on another talking horse, with the Doctor playing the trainer. He wants you to introduce him the same as Nino."

"Right you are," Matthew whispered back. "I've got the idea."

And when Jojo the dancing elephant had bowed himself out amidst a storm of applause, the ringmaster stepped to the entrance flap and himself led forward the next, the star, act.

For a moment old Beppo, accompanied by a short, stout man in cavalry uniform, seemed a little scared to find a sea of faces staring down at him.

Motioning to the strange-looking performers to remain by the edge of the ring a moment, Matthew advanced into the center. With a lordly wave of the hand he silenced the wheezy band who were still finishing Jojo's last dance. And in the quiet that followed he looked up at the audience and filled his lungs for his last and most impressive speech.

"Ladies and gentleman," roared Ringmaster Mugg, "we 'ave now harrived at the last and most himportant act in our long and helegant program. You 'ave all 'eard, I'm sure, of Nino—Nino, the world-famous talking horse, and his gallant owner, the dashing cossack cavalry officer, Captain Nicholas Pufftupski. There they are, ladies and gentlemen— you see them before you in the flesh. Kings and queens have traveled miles to witness their act. Only two months ago, when we were playing in Monte Carlo, we 'ad to turn away the Prime Minister of England because we 'adn't got a seat for 'im in the 'ouse."

"Oh, stop this nonsense, Matthew," whispered the Doctor, coming up to him, dreadfully embarrassed. "There's no need to—"

But the eloquent ringmaster hurried on with a thunderous voice:

"General Pufftupski is a modest man and he forbids me to tell you about 'is medals what was given 'im by the King of Sweden and the Empress of China. I now pass on to the hextraordinary hintelligence of the animal you see before you. On 'is way back from chasing Napoleon out of Russia, Count Pufftupski was took prisoner—and 'is 'orse, the famous Nino, with 'im. During their himprisonment they became very hintimate. So much so that at the end of the two years while they was captives of the French, Nino and 'is owner could talk to one another freely—the same as you and I might do. If you don't believe what I say, you can prove it for yourselves. All you 'ave to do is to ask any question of Nino through his owner and it will be answered—if it 'as an answer. Field Marshal Pufftupski will open 'is performance with this marvelous 'orse with a few tricks just to show you what they can do. Ladies and gentlemen, I 'ave great pleasure in introducing to you the Archduke Nicholas Pufftupski, Commander-in-Chief of the Russian Army, and 'is battle charger, the one and only, world-famous NINO."

As the band played a few opening chords the Doctor and Beppo stepped forward to the center of the ring and bowed. A tremendous burst of applause came from the people.

It was a strange performance, the only one of its kind ever given to a circus audience. The Doctor, when he entered the ring, had no definite idea of what he was going to do. Neither had Beppo. But the old, old veteran knew that the performance was going to win him comfort and freedom from work for the rest of his days. Every once in a while during the course of the act he would forget his noble ancestry and slump back into his usual weary, worn-out appearance. But on the whole, as Hop said afterward, he made a much better-looking show horse than anyone had

" 'The Commander-in-Chief of the Russian Army' "

expected; and so far as the audience was concerned, his success surpassed anything Blossom had ever exhibited.

After doing a few tricks, Colonel Pufftupski turned to the
people and offered (in remarkably good English) to make
the horse do anything they asked. Immediately a little boy
in the front row cried out, "Tell him to come over here and
take my hat off."

The Doctor made a sign or two and Beppo went straight
to the boy, lifted the cap from his head, and put it into his
hand. Then numberless questions were shouted by the audience, and to every one Beppo gave an answer—sometimes

by tapping the floor, sometimes by shaking his head, and sometimes by word of mouth, which the Doctor translated. The people enjoyed it so much that Blossom, watching through a slit outside, thought they'd never be done. And when at last the gallant Pufftupski led his horse out of the ring the audience clapped and cheered and called to him again and again to come back and receive their applause.

The news of the wonderful success of the circus's first performance in Bridgeton, mostly brought about by the marvelous talking horse, quickly spread through the town. And long before the evening show was due people were lined up outside the big tent, four deep, waiting patiently to make sure of seats, while the rest of the enclosure and all the side shows were packed and thronged so tight that you could hardly move through the crowds.

· The Sixth Chapter ·

BEPPO THE GREAT

THE money, over which poor Dab-Dab had so worried, was soon replaced in the Dolittle savings box. During the days at Bridgeton the throngs that crowded into the enclosure left so many sixpences at the booth of the two-headed animal from the jungles of Africa that Too-Too prophesied the record of the Ashby week would be easily beaten.

"I estimate, Doctor," said he, putting his mathematical head on one side and closing his left eye, "that in six days we should easily make sixteen pounds—and that's not allowing for any extra business on the market day or Saturday."

"And most of that you can put down to the Doctor's act with Beppo," said Jip. "If it wasn't for that act, and the talk it has made, the crowds wouldn't be half as big."

Finding what a success John Dolittle's performance was making, Blossom came to him after the first showing and begged him to keep it up for the whole of the week that the circus stayed at Bridgeton.

"Well, but look here," said John Dolittle, "I've promised

Beppo that he would be pensioned off for obliging you in your emergency. I don't know how soon Nino will be able to work again, but I did not say anything to Beppo about acting all week. I supposed you would put something else on in our place as soon as you had time to look around."

"Good Lord, Doctor!" said Blossom. "I couldn't find anything to take the place of your act if I looked around for a year. There's never been anything like it since the circus was invented. The news of it has gone all over the town— and a good ways outside of it, too. They say folks are coming all the way from Whittlethorpe to see your act. Listen, can't you ask Beppo to oblige us? It ain't heavy work for 'im. Tell 'im we'll give 'im anything 'e likes—asparagus for breakfast and a featherbed to sleep in—if 'e only says the word. My outfit, with the sideshows and all, is taking in pretty near fifty pounds a day now. Never saw such business! If this keeps up we shan't 'ave to stay in the game long before we're all on easy street."

There was something of contempt in the Doctor's face as he looked at Blossom and paused a moment before he answered.

"Oh, yes," he said rather sadly, "you're willing enough to treat your poor old servant well now, aren't you?—now he is bringing you in money. For years and years he has worked for you and never even got his coat brushed in return—just enough hay and oats to keep him going. Now you'll give anything in the world. Money! Bah! It's a curse."

"Well," said Blossom, "I'm helping to make up for it now, ain't I? It ain't 'eavy work, answering questions and doin' tricks. You go and talk to 'im, Doctor. Lord bless me! Don't it sound queer?—me asking you to go and talk to 'im—and twenty-four hours ago I didn't know there ever was such a thing as talking to 'orses!"

"Except with a whip," said John Dolittle. "I wish I could put you in his place and make you work thirty-five years for Beppo in return for hay and water and a lot of beating and neglect. All right, I'll put your request before him and see what he says. But remember, his decision is to be final. If he refuses to give one single performance more I shall hold you to your promise—a comfortable home for him and a good pasture to graze in for the rest of his life. And I almost hope he'll say no."

The Doctor turned on his heel and, leaving the ringmaster's wagon, set off toward the stables.

"Poor old Beppo!" he murmured. "His ancestor carried Julius Caesar in military reviews—heard the legions cheer the conqueror of the world, who sat astride his back! Poor old Beppo!"

When he entered the stables he found the wagon horse gazing out of the window of his stall at the pleasant fields that lay beyond the circus enclosure.

"Is that you, John Dolittle?" said he, as the Doctor opened the door. "Have you come to take me away?"

"Beppo," said John Dolittle, putting his hand on the veteran's gaunt and bony back, "it seems you are now a great man—I mean a great horse."

"How's that, Doctor? I don't understand."

"You've become famous, Beppo. This is a funny world. And we humans, I often think, are the funniest animals in it. Mr. Blossom has just found out, after you have been in his service for thirty-five years, how valuable and intelligent you are."

"In what way valuable?"

"Because you talk, Beppo."

"But I've always talked."

"Yes, I know. But Mr. Blossom and the world *didn't* know

until I proved it to them in the circus ring. You have made a great sensation, Beppo, just on the eve of your retirement. Now, they don't want you to retire. They want you to continue being wonderful—just talking, the way you've always done."

"It sounds crazy, doesn't it Doctor?"

"Perfectly. But you have suddenly become so valuable to Blossom that he will give you asparagus for breakfast, a valet to brush your coat, and another to curl your mane if you'll only stay and act for him for the rest of the week."

"Humph! That's what it means to be famous, does it? I'd sooner be turned out into a nice big field."

"Well, Beppo, you are to suit yourself—at last, after thirty-five years of suiting other people. I've told Blossom I'm going to hold him to his bargain. If you don't want to do it, say so. You shall retire today if you wish."

"What would you advise me to do, Doctor?"

"There is this about it," said John Dolittle, "if you give Blossom what he wants now, we may be able to get you what you want—that is, more exactly what you want—later. You see, he has no farm of his own to put you on; he would have to get a farmer to graze you and take care of you for him. And besides, he will probably be better disposed toward me and some plans I have for the other animals."

"All right, Doctor," said Beppo. "Then that settles it. I'll do it."

There was no happier man in the world than Alexander Blossom when John Dolittle came and told him that Beppo had consented to act all the week. He at once got handbills printed and had them sent to the neighboring towns and given away in the streets. These told the public that the world-famous talking horse was to be seen at Bridgeton for only four remaining days, and that those who did not wish

"He had handbills given away in the streets"

to miss the chance of a lifetime had better hurry up and come to Blossom's Mammoth Circus.

Nothing succeeds like success. It was only necessary to have the news go through the town that people were being turned away, to make twice the number clamor for admission. "Bridgeton week" came to be spoken of among the showfolk for a long time afterward as the outstanding period in the circus's whole career.

· The Seventh Chapter ·

THE PERFECT PASTURE

IN the meantime John Dolittle was making Blossom fulfill the other parts of his bargain. It was not long after the circus had opened at Bridgeton that the elephant sent Jip for the Doctor because he was suffering from an acute attack of rheumatism—brought on by living in an exceedingly damp and dirty stable.

The poor creature was in considerable pain. The Doctor, after examining, prescribed massage. Blossom was sent for and ordered to buy a barrel of a special costly kind of balm. A few weeks before, of course, the ringmaster would have flatly refused to go to such an expense for his animals' comfort. But now, with John Dolittle bringing him in the biggest business that his show had ever seen, he was ready to do almost anything to please him. The balm was sent for right away and then the Doctor demanded six strong men to help him.

Massaging an elephant is no light work. A large audience gathered in the menagerie to watch the six men and the Doctor crawling over the elephant's body, rubbing and pummeling the ointment into his hide till the sweat ran from their foreheads.

"Massaging the elephant"

Then the Doctor ordered a new stable built for the big creature, with a special kind of wooden floor with drainage under it and a lot of other up-to-date features. And, although this work was also expensive, carpenters were brought in and it was completed in three hours. The result was that the elephant got well in a very short time.

The Doctor also drew up rules for the menagerie keeper that improved the condition of all the other animals. And in spite of the fact that the keeper grumbled a good deal about "running a zoo like a beauty parlor," Blossom made him understand that he would be discharged immediately if the Doctor's new regulations were not strictly obeyed.

Poor Nino was still pretty sick. He was getting better, but his recovery was dreadfully slow. The Doctor visited him twice a day. But Blossom now realized that the cob's act, which had always been done under his own guidance, could never take the place of the far finer performance of Beppo and the Doctor. Beppo, his age and appearance notwithstanding, was a much cleverer horse than Nino.

Well, the week wore on toward its end. John Dolittle had made arrangements with Blossom that after the last performance on Saturday he and Beppo were to leave and go away to a certain farmer who had agreed to keep the old horse in good grazing for the remainder of his days. He was to have all the oats he wanted and white radishes (a delicacy that Beppo was particularly fond of) twice a week. The Doctor and Beppo were going to inspect this farm, and if they didn't like it, another one to their satisfaction was to be found.

The last performance was over; the big tent was being pulled down, and the Doctor and Beppo were all ready for their departure. The old horse's luggage consisted of a blanket (a new one the Doctor had made Blossom buy as a farewell present), which he wore. The Doctor's luggage was his little black bag and a small bundle, which was also carried on Beppo's back. John Dolittle was standing at the gate, his hand on Beppo's bridle waiting for Matthew, who had run back to the wagon to get some sandwiches, which Dab-Dab was preparing.

Presently he saw Blossom hurrying across the enclosure in a great state of excitement. A little way behind walked a short, very smartly dressed man.

"Listen, Doc," panted the ringmaster coming up, "I've just

had the biggest offer I ever got in my life. That toff coming along is the proprietor of the Manchester Amphitheater. He wants my outfit to show in his theater—one of the biggest in the country—week after next. And 'e specially wants Beppo. What do you think he guarantees us? A hundred pounds a day! And maybe more if—"

"No!" the Doctor interrupted firmly, holding up his hand. "Beppo may not have many more years to live, but what he has he's going to spend in comfort. Tell that to your manager. Beppo retires—today—from the circus business for good."

And without waiting for his sandwiches, he led the old horse out of the enclosure and hurried down the road.

Beppo and John Dolittle had not gone very far before they were overtaken by Too-Too.

"Doctor," said the owl, "I came after you to let you know about the money."

"Too-Too," John Dolittle replied, "at the present moment the subject of money is more than usually distasteful to me. Beppo and I are trying to get away from the very smell of it."

"But just think what you can *do* with money, Doctor," said Too-Too.

"Yes, that's the trouble with the beastly stuff. It's the power of it that makes it such a curse."

"Dab-Dab asked me," Too-Too went on, "to come and let you know how much the pushmi-pullyu had made this week at Bridgeton because she thought perhaps you might think of retiring to Puddleby when you heard. I only just got it figured out—deducting Blossom's share and the bills we owe the tradespeople. It was a big piece of arithmetic, I can tell you. My estimate was way off. Instead of sixteen pounds, we made twenty-six pounds, thirteen shillings, and tenpence, clear profit."

"Humph," murmured the Doctor. "It's a large amount, but not enough for us to retire on, Too-Too. Still, it would go quite a long way toward it. Tell Dab-Dab to keep it safe for me and we will talk over the matter when I get back. I am returning tomorrow, you know. Good-bye—and thank you very much for bringing me the news."

Now, the Doctor had in his pocket the address of the farmer to whom they were going. Imagine his surprise on reaching his destination to find that it was the same farm as the one where his old friend, the plow horse, lived!

There were hearty greetings, a good deal of astonishment, and much joy at the meeting. The old plow horse, beaming through his green spectacles, was introduced to Beppo, and Beppo was introduced to him. It was curious that although the Doctor had known the plow horse for so long he had never heard his name. And it was only on introducing the two old horses to one another that he learned it for the first time. It was Toggle.

"You know," said the plow horse, "I am tremendously glad to see you both, but I am a little sorry, for Beppo's sake, that it was to this farm that Blossom sent him. The farmer himself is a very decent fellow, but this pasture I have here leaves a good deal to be desired."

"But we don't *have* to stay here," said the Doctor. "I told Blossom that if it did not meet with Beppo's approval he must find another. In what way is this place unsuitable? Is the grass bad?"

"No," said Toggle, "the grass is all right—a little rank in August if there's much rain, but it's sweet enough most of the year. But the meadow slopes the wrong way. You see, this hillside is facing northeast. It's only in midsummer that

"The old plow horse was introduced to Beppo"

you get any sun. It stays behind the hill the rest of the year. Then the prevailing wind is a cold northeaster that blows across the meadow, and there's little protection from it—except along that hedge over there and one soon eats up that bit of grass."

"Well, tell me," said the Doctor, turning to Beppo, "what, for you, would be the ideal, the most attractive place for an old horses' home?"

"The place I've always dreamed of," said Beppo, gazing across the landscape with a wistful look in his old eyes, "is like this—part of it is sloping and part of it is flat. Slopes are such a nice change: the grass is nearer to your nose, and the flats are restful to get back to after the slopes. Then it has trees, big spreading trees with fat trunks—the kind horses love to stand under and think—after a hearty meal. It has a copse where herds and wild roots grow, the sorts we love to nibble for a change—especially wild mint, which is soothing to the stomach when you've eaten too much. It has good water—not a muddy little pond, but a decent brook where the water is always sparkling and clear. In a hollow it has a nice old shelter with a dry floor and a mossy, tiled roof that doesn't let the rain in. The pasture varies: some places are firm, croppy turf; others are deep, luscious, long hay-grass, with buttercups and fragrant wild flowers mixed in it. At the top of the hilly part you can get a view of the sunsets to the westward and the south. And on the summit there is a good firm post to scratch your neck on. I love to watch the sun go down as I scratch my neck of an evening. The whole place is protected with good fences from snappy dogs and worrisome people. It is quiet. It is peaceful. And that, John Dolittle, is the place where I would spend my old age."

"Humph!" murmured the Doctor when Beppo had ended. "Your description sounds delightful—almost like the place where I'd wish to spend my own old age—though I suppose I'd want a little more furniture than a scratching post. Toggle, do you know of a pasture such as this that Beppo speaks of?"

"I do, indeed, Doctor," said Toggle. "Come with me and I'll show you."

Then the plow horse led them over the brow of the hill and down the other side a way. Here, facing the sunny southward, they looked over a farm gate into the loveliest meadow you ever saw. It was almost as if some fairy had

"They looked over a wide farm gate"

made old Beppo's wish come true, for it was the retreat he had described in every detail: there was the clump of great elm trees; there was the copse and the sparkling brook; there was the snug shelter in the hollow; and on the summit of the slope, against the red glow of the setting sun, stood the post for Beppo to scratch his neck on.

"This is it, Doctor," said Beppo quietly. "This is the spot— just as I had always planned it. No horse could ask for any better place to pass his old age."

"It's wonderful," said the Doctor, himself entirely captivated by the beauty of the scene. "It has character, that meadow. Does this land belong to your farmer, Toggle?"

"No," said the plow horse. "I've often tried to break in here and graze. And I did get through the hedge once or twice, but the owner always chased me out again. It belongs to a farmer who lives in that little house down there with the red roof."

"I see," said the Doctor. "I wonder how much a piece of ground like that would cost."

"Not very much, I shouldn't think," said Toggle. "Although it is large, the farmer has never raised anything but hay on it."

"But, Doctor," said Beppo, "why buy it? I thought you said that Blossom was going to pay for my pensioning off."

"Yes," said the Doctor. "But he has only agreed to pay for your board and lodging. I've always had an idea I'd like to start a home for retired cab and wagon horses. And this place is such an ideal one for aged horses that I thought, if I could, I'd buy it. Then we would form The Retired Cab and Wagon Horses' Association and you could keep the place for your own, for good."

"What a marvelous idea!" cried both horses together.

"But have you got enough money, Doctor?" asked Beppo. "Jip often told me that you were as poor as a church mouse."

"That is so—more or less," the Doctor agreed. "Money with me has always been a most uncertain thing. But, as you heard Too-Too come and tell me shortly after we had left the circus, I am now some twenty-six pounds to the good. I owe a sailor a lot of money for a boat, but his need is not so urgent as your own—I sent a bird to find out, so I know. I can make some more money later on to pay him with. Of course, twenty-six pounds is not enough to buy a piece of land that big, outright. But perhaps the farmer will let me pay so much down and the rest by installments every year. If he will, it becomes yours right away and nobody can take it away from you—unless I fail in my payments. Now, you two wait here, and I'll go and see him about it."

Leaving the two horses by the gate, the Doctor set off across country for the little red-roofed house that Toggle had pointed out.

· The Eighth Chapter ·

THE RETIRED CAB AND
WAGON HORSES' ASSOCIATION

NOW, the farmer who owned the land which the Doctor wished to buy was, at the moment when John Dolittle knocked upon his door, sitting at his parlor table talking to Toggle's farmer. He was sorely in need of twenty pounds to buy seed potatoes with. But Toggle's farmer, with many apologies, had been compelled to refuse him because he himself was very short of money at this time. It was this conversation which the Doctor's call interrupted.

The farmer was very hospitable and invited John Dolittle to come in and sit down at the table with his other guest. Mugs of fragrant cider were brought in by the host's wife. Then the Doctor described the piece of ground that Toggle had shown him and asked if it was for sale. And as it was one which the farmer seldom used he immediately said yes, it was. For how much, the Doctor asked. For one hundred and twenty pounds, the farmer told him.

"Well," said the Doctor, "I only have twenty-six pounds at present. Suppose I gave you that down and promised to pay the rest in twenty-pound installments every six months: would you let me have it?"

The farmer, seeing a chance of getting his seed potatoes,

"John Dolittle knocked upon his door"

was going to agree at once, but the other, Toggle's farmer, broke into the conversation.

"What be you going to use the land for, stranger?" he asked. "You ain't thinkin' of puttin' up no glue factory, I hope."

"Oh, no," said the Doctor. "I want to make it into a rest farm for old horses—just a grazing ground. Practically nothing will be altered."

The two farmers thought the stranger must be crazy. But, as he and the plan he proposed seemed harmless enough, they readily gave in.

"By the way," said the Doctor, still speaking to Toggle's owner, "you have a friend of mine at your farm, a plow horse: he wears spectacles, which I gave him years ago when he lived in Puddleby."

"Oh, aye," said the farmer. "I know 'un—Toggle. A queer beast, that. 'E wouldn't be parted from them specs for anything. What about 'im?"

"He is too old to work, isn't he?" said the Doctor. "You let him graze now most of the time, I understand. He wishes to use this same pasture with the horse I have brought today. Will you let him?"

"That I will," said the farmer. "But how come you to know all this about my horse?"

"Oh, well," said the Doctor, looking sort of embarrassed, "I have ways of my own knowing what horses want. I'm a naturalist."

"Sounds like you was an *unnaturalist* to me," said the farmer, winking at his neighbor.

After a little discussion on how the first money would be sent, the bargain was closed and the Doctor was told that now, so long as his part of the arrangement was fulfilled, the land belonged to him.

"Not to me," he said as he rose and bade the farmers farewell. "The land belongs to the Association. I am turning it over to the horses themselves."

Having inquired of his host where he could find a carpenter, the Doctor left. And when, a half hour later, the two farmers walked across the field together they saw the strange naturalist and the carpenter busily putting up a large signboard in the middle of the pasture. On it was written in big letters:

REST FARM

THIS LAND IS THE PROPERTY OF THE RETIRED CAB AND
WAGON HORSES' ASSOCIATION. TRESPASSERS AND VICIOUS
DOGS WILL BE KICKED.

By ORDER,

(Signed, on behalf of the Committee.)

BEPPO, President.

TOGGLE, Vice President.

NOTE—MEMBERSHIP FREE
FOR ADMISSION APPLY AT THE GATE

Well, after seeing the first two members of the Association enter into possession of their new quarters, John Dolittle bade Beppo and Toggle farewell and set off on his return journey.

As he passed down the road he looked back many times to watch the two old veterans prancing around their beautiful new home. The sight warmed his heart and he smiled as he hurried on.

"I'm not sure," he murmured to himself, "but I think that is almost the best job I ever did. Poor creatures! They are happy at last, growing young again after a life of hard work. I must establish some more institutions like that. I've one or two in mind. The Rat and Mouse Club, for instance. I'd like to see that started. Of course, I shall get in a frightful row over this from Dab-Dab when she finds out that I've spent all the money again. Oh, well, it's worth it. I'll send some London cab horses down to join them as soon as I get to the city again. Humph"—the Doctor paused and looked back—"There they are—at it still—Beppo rolling down the hill and Toggle splashing through the brook . . . Great heavens! I forgot all about the radishes. Why didn't Beppo remind me?"

He hurried back. On the way he met a lad playing in the road. Questioning him, he found he was the son of the farmer who had sold the land.

"Would you like to earn a shilling a week?" asked the Doctor.

"I'd like to earn a shilling a month," said the boy. "I want to save up and buy some skates for next winter. I've got only ninepence so far."

"Do you know how to grow radishes?"

"Yes," answered the boy. "That's easy. They're about the only thing I can grow."

"Very good," said John Dolittle. "Now, you see that meadow where the horses are—and the shelter at the bottom? Well, I've just bought that land from your father. It's to be a home for horses. If you'll plant me a radish bed behind the shelter, the white kind, you know, I'll pay you a shilling a week for keeping it in order. Are you willing?"

"I should say I am, sir!" cried the boy.

"All right. Here's your first shilling—and here's a penny to buy a packet of seed with. I appoint you head gardener to the rest farm. You're now on the payroll of the Retired Cab and Wagon Horses' Association. Make the radish bed fairly big because I may be sending down some more horses later. When the radishes are ripe, you make them up into bunches and hand them out to the members twice a week. And don't forget to plant new seed every so often, to keep up the supply. Understand?"

"Yes, sir."

"Now give me your Christian name," said the Doctor, "and I'll send you your wages every week. And if you should

" 'Would you like to earn a shilling a week?' "

have to leave your job—to go away or anything—get your father to write me a letter. He knows how to reach me."

The boy, pleased as Punch with his good luck, gave the Doctor his name, took his money, and ran off to get a spade and fork and start his new work.

"Well, so that's that," the Doctor murmured as he hurried on toward Bridgeton. "Now, I must try to think out a way to break the news gently to Dab-Dab that our money box is emptied again."

The rest farm that the Doctor established that day continued to flourish and grow for many years. And another worry was added to the many which harassed Dab-Dab, the careful housekeeper. For not only had the Doctor bound himself to send the farmer twenty pounds every six months, but he further reduced the Dolittle fortunes by buying, every once in a while, some specially old and weary horse that he would meet on the streets. He bought them from cab drivers, from rag-and-bone men, from all sorts of people. Poor Dab-Dab used to be terrified when she saw a Gypsy wagon come in sight on the road. For Gypsies' horses were always particularly thin and scrawny-looking, and it was almost certain that the Doctor would try to buy the poor creatures from men who were much better skilled than he in shrewd bargaining.

All these old waifs and wrecks of horses the Doctor would send down to the rest farm to be made free members of the Association. Beppo's and Toggle's partnership grew into quite a family circle of old cronies—horses from all walks of life. And many were the interesting tales of bygone days told beneath the big trees of an evening or around the post on top of the hill. Here the old fellows would stand in line, waiting to scratch their necks, watching the beauty of the peaceful landscape grow dim in the red glow of the setting sun.

And still the membership list grew longer and longer. The boy who kept the radish garden sent a letter to the Doctor, saying he had had to enlarge the bed and needed help. He had a school friend, he wrote, who was also saving up to buy skates. Would the Doctor employ him, too?

The Doctor did; and the payroll of the Association advanced to two shillings a week. John Dolittle paid a visit to the farm after it had been going for about three months. On consulting with the committee (five of the oldest veterans), he found that money was required for repairing fences and keeping the ditches clear beneath the hedges. Some of the

HUGH LOFTING

" 'What's the use?' cried Too-Too"

members needed their hoofs trimmed (they didn't bother to wear shoes, of course). So he arranged with the lad he had first appointed as gardener to extend the radish bed considerably, in order that quite a large crop of vegetables could be grown—more than was needed for the members.

The lad had a good head for business and this was done; and two more friends of his were employed for the extra work. Then the money that was made by selling the vegetables was used to form a Fencing and Farriers' Fund, to hire hedgers and ditchers and blacksmiths every so often to keep the fences in repair and to trim the members' roofs.

Paying the extra boys, of course, took still more from the Dolittle money box—and added still more to the worries of Dab-Dab the housekeeper.

"What's the use?" cried Too-Too one evening when they were discussing accounts. "What's the use of my doing all this double-entry bookkeeping—making my head fairly ache with arithmetic? It doesn't do any good to calculate how much the Doctor has—or to estimate how much he's going to have. No matter what it is, he spends it all!"

PART V

· The First Chapter ·

MR. BELLAMY OF MANCHESTER

Y getting a lift on the road, John Dolittle reached the circus late that night instead of early the following morning, as he had expected. And the first thing that Matthew Mugg said to him as he entered the wagon was, "Blossom told me he wanted to see you as soon as you got in. That toff from Manchester is still with him."

Thereupon the Doctor immediately left his own wagon and set out for that of the ringmaster. Jip asked could he come along, and the Doctor said yes.

The circus was now all packed up ready for departure early tomorrow morning. As John Dolittle approached Blossom's caravan he saw a light in the window. It was very late —after midnight.

Within, he found the ringmaster sitting at the little table with the smartly dressed man whom he had seen earlier in the day.

"Good evening, Doctor," said the ringmaster. "This gentleman is Mr. Frederick Bellamy, proprietor and manager of the Manchester Amphitheater. He has something 'e'd like to say to you."

The Doctor shook hands with Mr. Bellamy, who at once

leaned back in his chair, put his thumbs in the armholes of his white waistcoat, and began:

"I have delayed my return to Manchester, Doctor Dolittle —in spite of urgent and pressing business—in order to discuss with you an engagement that I had offered to Mr. Blossom this afternoon. I witnessed your act with the talking horse and was greatly interested in it. Mr. Blossom tells me that he tried to get you to consent to take part in his show's performance in my theater, but that you refused—took the horse away to put him grazing."

The Doctor nodded, and Mr. Bellamy went on:

"I then supposed that the deal was off, because—I don't mind telling you—without your act I would not be interested in this circus. But Mr. Blossom has persuaded me to remain and talk with you myself. He assured me that the intelligence of the performance was not in that particular horse, but in your own unusual powers with animals—that you could give as good a show with any horse. He tells me, though I confess I can hardly believe it, that you can actually communicate with animals in their own language. Is that so?"

"Well," said the Doctor, looking uncomfortable, "I'm sorry that Mr. Blossom told you this. I don't claim it or talk of it myself because I find that people don't usually believe me. But . . . yes, it is true. With most animals I can converse freely."

"Indeed," said Mr. Bellamy. "Most extraordinary! That being the case, we had thought that perhaps you would be willing to do us an act with some other animal, or animals, in place of the horse that you have just taken away. My idea is to make it something more elaborate—to have it form the bigger, more important part of Mr. Blossom's show. It is something quite new, this gift of yours. And, properly put on, it ought to make a great sensation. Of course, you understand, it would be well paid for—very, I might say. Would you consider it?"

"I haven't any other act worked out at the moment," said the Doctor. "I am somewhat new to this business. My idea of shows with animals is that they must always be done with the consent and willing cooperation of the animals themselves."

"Oh, quite, quite," said Mr. Bellamy. "It is very late now. Suppose you think it over until tomorrow. I cannot catch the coach tonight. And if you consider it, let me know in the morning, eh?"

When the Dolittle household awoke next morning they found that the wagon was moving. This was nothing new for them. It only meant that the circus had got underway very early while they were still asleep—as it often did in moving from town to town. It was a part of the life, this, that Gub-Gub greatly enjoyed—waking in the morning and looking out of the window to see what kind of new scene lay around their moving home.

Gub-Gub used to boast that this showed he was a born traveler, that he loved change, like the Doctor. As a matter of fact, he was really by nature much more like Dab-Dab, for no one loved regular habits, especially regular meals, more than he. It was just that the Gypsy life provided a continuous and safe sort of adventure for him. He liked excitement, but comfortable excitement, without hardship or danger. Matthew Mugg came in while the family was still at breakfast.

"Doctor," said he, "that Mr. Bellamy is still with the outfit. Said he might as well come along with us, as we was going the same way as him. But, if you ask me, I reckon the real reason is because he's afraid he may lose sight of you. He's just crazy to get you to perform at his theater—don't care

HUGH LOFTING

"It was a part of the life Gub-Gub greatly enjoyed"

nothin' about the rest of Blossom's show. But he's willin' to pay any amount to get you to give a performance of your own with animals."

"Well," said the Doctor, "it isn't as easy as it sounds, Matthew. My own pets here are anxious to do a play. I wrote a sort of comedy last night after they had gone to bed. But, of course, it will have to be rehearsed. The animals must know their parts properly. You might go forward and tell him that I will let him see it tomorrow, if we are far enough on with it."

"All right," said Matthew, and he stepped out of the back of the moving wagon and ran forward to overtake the ringmaster's caravan with his message.

Doctor Dolittle had written plays before for animals—dozens of them. I have told you of his very famous little book called *One-Act Plays for Penguins*. He had also written longer dramas for monkeys and others. But all these had been intended for audiences of animals and were written in animal languages. The penguin plays were performed during the long winter nights, where the birds sit around on the rocks in solemn groups, clapping their flipperlike wings when anything said by the actors strikes them as particularly sensible.

The plays for monkeys were of a much lighter kind. They preferred comedies to the more serious dramas that the penguins liked.

So, you see, John Dolittle was quite experienced as a playwright for animals. But the thing needed by Mr. Bellamy, which was to be shown to an audience of people, had to be different because people don't understand animal languages. And after much thought the Doctor decided to do away with language altogether. The whole play was to be action. And he called it *The Puddleby Pantomime*.

The rehearsals for the pantomime were greatly enjoyed by everyone except Dab-Dab. The poor housekeeper, who had herself a part to play in it, was continually stopping the performance to row with someone about upsetting the furniture or breaking the teacups or pulling down the curtains.

The pantomime was just like the old-fashioned Harlequinade, a funny musical play about two men who both love and fight for Columbine. Also in the play is a policeman chasing a thief, who has stolen a string of sausages. Toby played the part of Harlequin, Dab-Dab was Columbine, Gub-Gub was

Pantaloon, Swizzle was the policeman, and Jip was Pierrot. The dance by Harlequin, Columbine, and Pierrot caused a lot of merriment because whenever the dancers were on the tips of their toes, that was certain to be the time when the wagon would give an extra bad lurch and throw the dancers under the bed.

Swizzle, as the policeman, was always arresting poor Pierrot (Jip) and anybody else he met. For a club he used a cucumber—until he broke it in half over Pantaloon (Gub-Gub), whom he was supposed to chase all around the wagon for stealing the string of sausages. Then the prisoner took the policeman's club away from him and ate it. And the Doctor decided to put that idea into the real show and to use a cucumber in Manchester.

Coming on and off the "stage" was very difficult because the performers had to go out of the door and stand on the narrow steps while the wagon was still going. Gub-Gub, in his part of the comic Pantaloon, had a hard time. He had to make many entrances and many exits—bounding in and out with the red-hot poker or the string of sausages. And in spite of the Doctor's warning him repeatedly to go out carefully, he always forgot that the wagon was moving, and, making his flying exit, he almost invariably fell out of the wagon, upside down, into the road. Then the rehearsal would have to be stopped while Mr. Pantaloon picked himself up and ran after his moving theater to get on the stage again.

The piece was gone through four or five times during that morning while the circus was traveling on to the next town. And when the train of wagons halted for the night the Doctor sent word to Mr Bellamy that, although the act was still very imperfect and no costumes ready yet, he could come and see if it would do.

"The pantomime was performed by the side of the road"

Then the pantomime was performed again, this time on the solid ground by the side of the road, before an audience of Mr. Bellamy, Blossom, Matthew Mugg, and the strong man. On this stage that stood still instead of lurching from side to side, the piece went much better; and, although Pantaloon got a bit mixed up and popped on and off the stage many times too often, the audience clapped loud and long when it was over and declared it one of the most amusing shows they had ever seen. "Perfectly splendid!" cried Mr. Bellamy. "It's just the thing we want. With a little more rehearsing and proper clothes, that should make a great hit.

Nobody can say this act is not enjoyed by the animals that take part in it. Now, I'm going on to Manchester this evening. And after Mr. Blossom has played his week in Little Plimpton he'll bring you on to my theater to open the beginning of the following week, Monday the seventeenth. In the meantime, I'll do some advertising. And I think we can promise you an audience worth playing to."

Theodosia Mugg was very busy during these days, making the costumes. Fitting suits of clothes to animals is not easy. Gub-Gub gave the most trouble. At the first dress rehearsal he came on with his suit upside down, and his wig back-to-front. He had his hind legs through the sleeves of the coat, wearing them as pants. His makeup, too, gave a lot of extra work to the stage manager. Mr. Pantaloon liked the taste of grease paint and he would keep licking his chops during the performance. So of course the rouge on his cheeks very soon got smeared all around his mouth and made him look as though he had been eating bread and jam.

But Pantaloon's greatest trial was his trousers. At first he fastened his trousers with a belt. But his stomach was so round and smooth that his belt would keep slipping off it. Whenever he ran on to the stage he would lose his pants on the way and arrive wearing only a coat and a wig. Then Theodosia made a special pair of suspenders for him to keep his pants up with, and the Doctor always inspected his dressing himself.

A similar accident happened frequently at the beginning to Dab-Dab. Theodosia had made her a very cunning little ballet skirt of stiff pink net. But the first time she wore it, doing an especially high kick in her dance with Harlequin, she kicked her skirt right over her partner's head. The excitement was added to considerably when Pantaloon, who had just rushed in, picked up the skirt and put it on

"He would arrive on the stage
wearing only a coat and a wig"

himself in place of the pants he had lost in his hurried entrance.

Many times the Doctor was in despair over the costuming part of it. However, Theodosia worked out a lot of very cunning dodges, by means of secret buttons, hooks, elastics and tapes, to hold the clothes and hats and wigs in place. Then by making the actors wear their costumes all day long the Doctor finally got his performers so they could move and run and dance in clothes as easily as they could without them.

· The Second Chapter ·

THE POSTER AND THE STATUE

THE day the circus moved to Manchester was a great one for the Dolittle household. None of the animals except Jip had been in a really large city before. On the way there Gub-Gub was constantly at the window of the caravan, watching the road and shouting out words over his shoulder to the others when anything new or wonderful came in sight.

Mr. Bellamy's showplace was a big amusement park, with all sorts of sideshows of its own and a large theater building in the center. Prizefights, wrestling matches, brass-band contests and all manner of entertainments were held in a large open-air place behind the theater. It was oval in shape and had seats banked up high all around it. This it was that had given it its name, the Amphitheater, because it was like the great open-air theaters of the Romans.

To Mr. Bellamy's amusement park the citizens of Manchester came out in thousands when they were in need of recreation—especially Saturday afternoons and in the evenings. At night the whole place was lit up with strings of little lights, and very gay and pretty it looked.

The park was so big that Blossom's Mammoth Circus could fit into one corner of it and not be seen. The ringmaster was greatly impressed.

"Lor' bless me," he said to the Doctor, "this is the way to run the show all right—on a grand scale. Bellamy must be rolling in money. Why, the theater building alone could hold three times as many people as we can fit into our big tent!"

Blossom's circus party, feeling dreadfully small and unimportant in such a huge concern, was guided to a place where it could halt and settle down. Shortly after the horses were stabled, the great Mr. Bellamy himself turned up. The first thing he inquired for was the Puddleby pantomime troupe.

"As for the rest of your show," he said to Blossom, "I'll leave you this corner of the grounds, and you can set up and do what business you can on your own. We get the biggest crowds after five o'clock in the evening and all Saturday afternoon—when we usually run a prizefight over in the arena. But Doctor Dolittle's company I am going to take care of separately. Of course, I'll pay the money through you, as I told you, and you divide it in whatever way you two arrange. But from now on he and his animals are under my management, you understand, and are not to be interfered with by anybody else. That's what we agreed on, isn't it?"

Then while Blossom and his men got their own sideshows set up, the Dolittle household and its wagon were taken off to another part of the grounds—close to the theater—and given a space within a high fence, where they could settle down in comfort.

Here they found a few other tents and caravans, the homes of various special performers taking part in the daily, or rather nightly, show that was given in the theater. Dancers they were, tight-rope walkers, singers, and what-not.

After the beds were made up and the Dolittle wagon put in order, the Doctor suggested a walk through the city. Jip and Gub-Gub at once asked could they come, and the Doctor consented. Dab-Dab thought she ought to remain behind and finish unpacking and get food cooked for supper.

Then when the Doctor had been over to make sure that Matthew Mugg had gotten the pushmi-pullyu comfortably settled he set out, accompanied by Gub-Gub and Jip, to see the sights of Manchester.

To reach the city proper they had to walk about half a mile through districts of ordinary houses and gardens that surrounded the big town.

Of course, John Dolittle and Jip, having been in London more than once, knew what a regular city looked like. But Gub-Gub, when they entered the thronged streets, teeming with traffic, bordered by grand shops and buildings, was greatly impressed.

"What a lot of people!" he murmured, his eyes nearly popping out of his head. "And just look at the cabs! I didn't know there were so many in the world—following one another down the street like a parade. And such splendid vegetable shops! Did you *ever* see such enormous tomatoes! Oh, I like this place. It's much bigger than Puddleby, isn't it? And much livelier. Yes, I like this town."

They came to an open place, a big square, with especially fine stone buildings on all sides of it. Gub-Gub wanted to know all about each of them, and the Doctor had to explain what a bank was, and a corn exchange and a municipal hall, and many more.

HUGH LOFTING

"He set out to see the sights of Manchester"

"And what's that?" asked Gub-Gub, pointing to the middle of the square.

"That's a statue," said the Doctor.

It was a very grand monument of a man on horseback. And Gub-Gub asked who he was.

"That's General Slade," said the Doctor.

"But why do they put a statue up to him?"

"Because he was a famous man," answered the Doctor. "He fought in India—against the French."

They passed out of this square and a little farther on

entered another, a smaller one, with no statue in it. As they were crossing it Gub-Gub suddenly stopped dead.

"Great heavens, Doctor!" he cried. "Look!"

At the far side of the square, on a hoarding, was an enormous poster—a picture of a pig dressed as Pantaloon, holding a string of sausages.

Why, it's *me*, Doctor!" said Gub-Gub, hurrying toward it.

And sure enough, written across the top in large letters was *The Puddleby Pantomime. A Mystery. Come and see the Unique Harlequinade. Bellamy's Amphitheater. Next Monday.*

The manager had been as good as his word. He had had an artist make pictures of the characters in the Doctor's play and posted them all over the city.

They couldn't get Gub-Gub away from it. The idea of coming into this big town and finding his own pictures on the walls and himself a famous actor already, entirely fascinated him.

"Perhaps they'll put up a statue of me next," he said, "—like the general. Look, there's room for one here. They haven't got any in this square."

As they went through the streets they found more pictures of their show—some of Dab-Dab, poised on her toes in a ballet skirt; some of Swizzle, with a policeman's helmet on his head. But whenever they passed one of Pantaloon they had the hardest work dragging Gub-Gub away. He would have sat in front of it all night, if they had let him, admiring himself as a famous actor.

"I really think you ought to speak to the mayor about my statue, Doctor," said he, as he sauntered homeward with his nose carried high in the air. "Perhaps they'll want to move the general into a smaller square and put me in the larger one."

On the morning of Monday, the day when the pantomime was to make its first appearance before the public, there was a dress rehearsal of it and the rest of the show to be given in the theater. This was what is known as a variety show. There were a number of different acts—dancers, singers, jugglers, and so forth. They came on to the stage in turn and went through their performance, with the orchestra playing the proper music for each one.

At the sides of the stage there were little frames, and at the beginning of each act footmen in livery came out and pushed big cards into them. These cards had the name of the new act on them, and were displayed in this way so that the audience could read what was coming. The Doctor suggested that with *The Puddleby Pantomime* the card changing should be done by animals, instead of footmen. Mr. Bellamy thought it was a splendid idea. And while the Doctor was wondering what animals he could get, Too-Too suggested that he be given the job.

"But we need two," said the Doctor. "You see how the footmen do it—like soldiers. They march out with the cards in their hand—just as though they were drilling, go to each side of the stage—pull the old card out and stick the new one in."

"That's all right, Doctor," said Too-Too. "I can soon get another owl, and we'll make a better pair than those footmen. You wait till I take a hunt around the country outside the city."

Too-Too flew off, and before half an hour had passed he was back again, with another owl who was the dead image of himself, and the exact same size. Then stools were placed on the corners of the stage, so that the little birds could reach the frames and the owl footmen were drilled in their parts.

"The footman came out and pushed big cards into them"

Even the musicians in the orchestra, accustomed to see-ing wonderful things done on the stage, were astonished when Too-Too and his brother owl appeared from behind the curtains. They were really much smarter at the job than the footmen in velvet. Like two clockwork figures, they hopped onto the stools, changed the cards, bowed to the imaginary audience, and retired.

"My!" said the bass fiddler to the trombone player. "Did you ever see the like? You'd think they'd been working in a variety hall all their lives!"

Then the Doctor, who was himself quite a musician, discussed with the conductor what kind of music should be played while the pantomime was going on.

"I want something lively," said John Dolittle, "but very, very soft—pianissimo the whole time."

"All right," said the conductor. "I'll play you the thing we do for the tightrope walkers—sort of tense."

Then he tapped his desk with his baton to make the orchestra get ready, and played a few opening bars. It was exciting, trembly music, played very, very quietly. It made you think of fairies fluttering across lawns in the moonlight.

"That's splendid," said the Doctor, as the conductor stopped. "Now, when Columbine begins to dance I want the minuet from *Don Juan*—because that's the tune she has always practiced to. And every time Pantaloon falls down have the percussion give the bass drum a good bang, please."

Then *The Puddleby Pantomime* was gone through on a real stage, with a real orchestra and real scenery—the last dress rehearsal. Gub-Gub found the glare of the footlights dazzling and confusing. But he and all the actors had, by this time, done the piece so often that they could have played it in their sleep. And the show went with a dash from beginning to end, without a single accident or slip.

When it was over Mr. Bellamy said, "Just one thing more: When the audience is here, your actors will be called out before the curtain. You'll have to show them how to take the call."

Then the performers were rehearsed in bowing. The five of them trooped on again, hand in hand, bowed to the empty theater and trooped off.

In the course of their eventful lives the animals of Doctor Dolittle's household had had many exciting times. But I doubt if anything ever happened to them that they remembered longer or spoke of afterward more often than their first appearance before the public in the famous Puddleby pantomime.

I say famous because it did, in fact, become very famous. Not only was it reported in the newspapers of Manchester as a sensational success, but it was written up in those magazines devoted to stagecraft and theatrical news, as something entirely new to the show business. Lots of acts with animals dressed as people had been done before, of course —some very good. But in all of them the performers never knew just why they did the things they did or the meaning of most of their act. Whereas the Doctor, being able to converse with his actors in their own language, had produced a play which was entirely perfect, down to the smallest detail. For instance, he had spent days in showing Toby how to wink one eye, and still longer in getting Pantaloon to throw back his head and laugh like a person. Gub-Gub used to practice it in front of a mirror by the hour. Pigs have their own way of laughing, of course, which most people don't know of; and that is just as well because sometimes they find humans very amusing. But to have animals laughing and frowning and smiling at the right places in a play— perfectly naturally and exactly the way people would do it— was something that had never been seen on the stage before.

Good weather and Mr. Bellamy's advertising had brought a large crowd out to the amusement park Monday evening. Long before the show was due to start the theater was beginning to fill.

Of the Dolittle troupe, waiting their turn behind the scene, no one was more anxious than the Doctor himself. None of his animals, with the exception of Swizzle, had ever performed before a real audience before. And it did not follow

"Gub-Gub used to practice it by the hour"

that because they had acted all right with only Mr. Bellamy and a few others looking on, they would be just as good when facing a packed theater.

As he heard the first few notes of the orchestra tuning up their instruments the Doctor peeped through the curtain into the audience. He could see nothing but faces. There did not seem to be room to get another in anywhere, but still the people crowded up to the big entrances at the end of the long hall, trying to find standing room in the aisles—or even outside of the doorways, where, on tiptoe, they could still get a glimpse of the stage.

"Doctor," whispered Dab-Dab, who was also peeping, "this at last ought to make us rich. Blossom said that Mr. Bellamy had promised him one hundred pounds a day—and more, if the audiences were larger than a certain number. It would be impossible for it to be bigger than this. You couldn't get a fly into that theater, it's so packed. What are they stamping and whistling for?"

"That's because the show is late in beginning," said the Doctor, looking at his watch. "They're impatient. Oh, look out! Let's get off the stage. They're going to pull the curtain up. See, there's the singing couple in the wings, ready to do the first act. Come on, hurry! Where's Gub-Gub got to? I'm so afraid that wig of his will slip out of place . . . Oh, here he is. Thank goodness, it's all right—and his pants, too. Now, all of you stay here and keep together. Our show goes on as soon as this act is over. Stop licking your face, Gub-Gut, for heaven's sake! I won't have time to make you up again."

· The Third Chapter ·

FAME, FORTUNE—AND RAIN

STAGE Manager Dolittle's anxiety about his company's behavior before a real audience turned out to be unnecessary. The lights and the music and the enormous crowd, instead of scaring the animals, had the effect of making them act the better. The Doctor said afterward that they had never done as well in rehearsal.

As for the audience, from the moment that the curtain went up they were simply spellbound. At the beginning many people would not believe that the actors were animals. They whispered to one another that it must be a troupe of boys or dwarfs, with masks on their faces. But there could be no disguising the two little owls who had opened the show by marching out like soldiers with the announcement cards. And as the pantomime proceeded even the most unbelieving of the audience could see that no human actors, no matter how well trained and disguised, could move and look like this.

At first Gub-Gub was an easy favorite. His grimaces and antics made the audience rock with laughter. But when Dab-Dab came on, opinion was divided. Her dance with

Toby and Jip simply brought down the house, as the saying goes. She captivated everybody. And it was really marvelous, considering how ungainly she usually was in her movements, to see with what grace she did the minuet. The people clapped, stamped the floor, yelled "Encore!" and just wouldn't let the show go on till she had done her dance a second time.

Then a lady in the front row threw a bunch of violets onto the stage. Dab-Dab had never had flowers thrown at her before and didn't know what to make of it. But Swizzle, an old actor, understood. Springing forward, he picked up the bouquet and handed it with a flourish to Columbine.

"Bow!" whispered the Doctor from the wings in duck language. "Bow to the audience—to the lady who threw the bouquet!"

And Dab-Dab curtsied like a regular ballerina.

When the curtain came down at the end and the music of the orchestra blared out loud the applause was deafening. The company trooped on hand in hand and bowed again and again. And still the audience called them back. Then the Doctor made them take the calls separately. Gub-Gub did antics and made faces; Swizzle took off his helmet and bowed; Toby sprang into the air with harlequinish agility; Jip struck tragic Pierrot-like attitudes, and Dab-Dab once more brought down the house by pirouetting across the stage on her toes, flipping kisses to the audience with the tips of her wings.

More bouquets were thrown to Columbine and a bunch of carrots to Pantaloon—which he started eating before he left the stage.

Mr. Bellamy said he had never seen such enthusiasm in the theater since he had owned it. And he immediately

HUGH LOFTING

"Dab-Dab curtsied like a regular ballerina"

asked Blossom if he would be willing to renew the engagement for a second week.

When the other acts were over and the audience left the theater Gub-Gub went out into the hall to look at the stage from the seats. There he found many programs scattered around the floor. He asked the Doctor what they were. And he was delighted when he was shown his own name printed there as playing the part of Pantaloon.

"Humph!" said he, folding it carefully. "I must keep this. I think I'll put it in my menu album."

"Don't you mean your stamp album?" asked the Doctor.

"No," said Gub-Gub. "I gave up collecting stamps some time ago. I collect menus now. They're much better fun to look at."

The Dolittle household, now that they were encamped near the theater, did not see so much of their old friends of the circus. Nevertheless, the Doctor frequently went across the amusement park to see how Matthew and the pushmi-pullyu were getting on. And Hop the clown, Hercules, and the Pintos often visited the theater to see the pantomime and to make tea at the Dolittle wagon.

The extraordinary success of the Doctor's play continued throughout the week—the crowds growing greater, if anything, with each performance. It became necessary to secure seats a long way in advance if you wanted to see the show, a thing which had only happened once before at the Amphitheater when a world-famous violinist had played there.

Wealthy gentlemen and elegant ladies called at the Doctor's little wagon almost every evening to congratulate him and to see and pet his marvelous animal actors. Gub-Gub got frightfully conceited and put on no end of temperamental airs, often refusing to see his admirers if they called during the hour he was accustomed to take for his nap.

"Famous artists have to be very careful of themselves," he said. "I am only at home to callers between ten and twelve in the morning. You better have that printed in the newspapers, Doctor."

One lady brought an autograph album for him to sign, and, with the Doctor's help, he put a very clumsy *"G.G."* in it for her and the picture of a parsnip, which, he said, was his family crest.

Dab-Dab, although she had become just as famous, was much more easily interviewed by visitors. Immediately after each performance she could be seen bustling about her household duties in the wagon, often still wearing her ballet skirt while she made beds or fried potatoes.

"That pig makes me tired," she said. "What's the use of our putting on airs? None of us would be famous if it hadn't been for the Doctor. Any animal could do what we do if they had him to teach them. By the way, Doctor," she added, spreading the tablecloth for supper, "have you been to see Blossom about the money?"

"No," said the Doctor. "Why bother yet? The first week is hardly over. And I understand the pantomime is to run a second one. No, I haven't seen Blossom in—let me see—not in three days."

"Well, you ought to. You should go and get your share of the money every night."

"Why? Blossom is a trustworthy man."

"Is he?" said Dab-Dab, putting the saltcellars on the table. "Well, I wouldn't trust him farther than I could see him. If you take my advice, you'll get your money each night. There must be a lot owing to you, especially since they put the pantomime on twice a day instead of only in the evening."

"Oh, that's all right, Dab-Dab," said the Doctor. "Don't worry. Blossom will bring me the money as soon as he has his accounts straightened out."

The housekeeper during the next few days frequently asked John Dolittle to see about this matter, but he never would. And even after the first week was over and the second nearly so Blossom had not come forward with the Doctor's share, nor, indeed, was he often seen by any member of the Dolittle household. The pushmi-pullyu had also done well with his sideshow, and, as the money made by this was quite sufficient for living expenses, the easygoing Doctor, as usual, refused to worry.

Toward the end of the second week the fame of *The Puddleby Pantomime* had become so great and so many people had called to interview the Doctor and his company that it was decided to invite the public to tea.

Then for a whole morning the good housekeeper was more than usually busy. Over two hundred printed cards of invitation had been sent out. Mrs. Mugg was called in to help. A large number of small tables were set about the wagon: the inside of the caravan was decorated with flowers; lots of tea and cakes were prepared and at four o'clock on Saturday afternoon the gates of the little enclosure beside the theater were thrown open to visitors.

All the animals, some of them dressed in their pantomime costumes, then acted as hosts and sat around at the tables, sipping tea with the elegant ladies and gentlemen who were anxious to meet them. It was a farewell party, for the next day the whole of Blossom's circus was to leave. The mayor of the city came and the mayoress and a number of newspaper reporters, who made sketches in their notebooks of Hostess Dab-Dab pouring tea and Gub-Gub handing around cakes.

The next day, after one of the most successful visits of its career, the circus packed up and moved out of Manchester.

The town they went to was a small one, some twelve miles to the northeast. Rain began to fall as the wagons arrived at the showground and the work of setting up was very disagreeable for everyone. For, besides the wretched, steady drizzle, the dirt underfoot soon got worked up into mud with the constant tramping of feet.

The rain continued the next day and the next. This, of course, was a terrible thing for the circus business because nobody came to see the show.

"Well, never mind," said the Doctor, as his family sat

"Gub-Gub handing around cakes"

down to breakfast on the third rainy morning. "We made plenty of money in Manchester. That should tide us over a bad spell easily."

"Yes, but you haven't got that money yet, remember," said Dab-Dab, "though goodness knows I've told you often enough to ask Blossom for it."

"I saw him this morning," said John Dolittle, "just before I came in to breakfast. It's quite all right. He says it was such a large amount he was afraid to keep it on him or in his wagon. So he put it in a bank in Manchester."

"Well, why didn't he take it out of the bank when he left," asked Dab-Dab, "and give you half of it?"

"It was a Sunday," said the Doctor. "And, of course, the banks were closed."

"But what does he mean to do about it, then?" asked the housekeeper. "He isn't going to leave it there, is he?"

"He's going back today to fetch it. He was just starting off on horseback when I spoke to him. I didn't envy him his ride in the rain."

Now, running a circus in an expensive thing. The animals have to be fed, the workmen and performers have to be paid, and there are a whole lot of other expenses for which money must be handed out hourly. So that during these rainy days, when no people came and the enclosure stood wet and empty instead of making money, The Mammoth Circus was losing it every day—every hour, in fact.

Just as the Doctor finished speaking the menagerie keeper, with his coat collar turned up against the rain, poked his head in the door.

"Seen the boss anywhere around?" he asked.

"Mr. Blossom has gone into Manchester," said John Dolittle. "He expects to be back about two in the afternoon, he told me."

"Humph!" said the man. "That's a nuisance."

"Why?" asked the Doctor. "Is there anything I can do for you?"

"I want money for rice and hay—for the menagerie," said the keeper. "The boss said he'd give me some this morning. The corn dealer's brought the feed. 'E won't leave it unless he gets his money. And my animals need the stuff bad."

"Oh, I suppose it slipped Mr. Blossom's mind," said the Doctor. "I'll pay the bill for you and get it from him when he returns. How much is it?"

"Thirty shillings," said the keeper, "for two bales of hay and fifty pounds of rice."

"All right," said the Doctor. "Too-Too, give me the money box."

"There you are! There you are!" Dab-Dab broke in, her feathers all ruffled up with anger. "Instead of getting the money from Blossom that he owes you, you are paying his bills for him! The animals' feed isn't your concern. What's the use? What's the use? Blossom getting richer and you getting poorer; that's you all over."

"The animals must be fed," said the Doctor, taking the money from the box and giving it to the keeper. "I'll get it back, Dab-Dab. Don't worry!"

The rain grew heavier and heavier all that morning. This was the circus's fourth day in this town. Hardly a penny had been taken in at the gates since the tents had been set up.

The Doctor, ever since his performance with Beppo at Bridgeton, had been looked upon by the showfolk with an almost superstitious respect. Any man, they felt, who could talk the language of animals must know more about them than a mere ringmaster like Blossom. The Doctor had, little by little, made great changes throughout the management of the whole concern—though there still remained a tremendous lot that he wished to alter. Many of the performers had for some time considered him as the most important man in the circus and Blossom as just a figurehead.

The menagerie keeper had hardly left before another man turned up wanting money for some other of the daily expenses of the show. And throughout that morning people kept coming to the Doctor with tales that Blossom had promised them payment at a certain time. The result, of course, was that before long the Dolittle money box (which had been quite well filled by the pushmi-pullyu's exhibition the last two weeks) was empty once more.

Two o'clock in the afternoon came—three o'clock—and still Mr. Blossom hadn't returned.

"Oh, he must have been delayed," said the Doctor to Dab-Dab, who was getting more anxious and more angry every minute. "He'll be here soon. He's honest. I'm sure of that. Don't worry."

At half past three Jip, who had been out nosing around in the rain, suddenly rushed in.

"Doctor!" he cried. "Come over to Blossom's wagon. I think there's something wrong."

"Why, Jip? What's the matter?" said the Doctor, reaching for his hat.

"Mrs. Blossom isn't there," said Jip. "At first I thought the door was locked. But I pushed it, and it wasn't. There's nobody in it. His trunk is gone—and nearly everything else, too. Come over and look. There's something queer about this."

· The Fourth Chapter ·

MR. BLOSSOM'S
MYSTERIOUS DISAPPEARANCE

JIP'S words brought a puzzled frown into the Doctor's face. Slowly he put on his hat and followed the dog out into the rain.

On reaching Blossom's wagon he found everything as Jip had described it. There was no one within. Every article of value had been taken away. A few torn papers lay scattered on the floor. In the inner room, Mrs. Blossom's private boudoir, the same situation met the Doctor's eyes. The whole place looked as though those who lived there had left in a hurry, to be gone a long time.

While John Dolittle was still gazing confusedly around him someone touched him on the shoulder from behind. It was Matthew Mugg.

"Looks kind of bad, don't it?" he said. "Blossom didn't have to take his trunk and all to go and get his money out of the bank. If you was to ask me, I've a kind of a notion that we ain't goin' to see our good, kind manager no more. Eh?"

"Well, Matthew," said the Doctor, "we mustn't jump to conclusions. He said he'd be back. He may have been delayed. As to his trunk and things, they're his own. He has a right to do what he wants with them. It would be wrong to pass any judgments until we have more evidence than that."

"Humph!" muttered the cat's-meat man. "O' course, you always did hate to think anybody crooked. Still, I think you can say good-bye to the money you earned in Manchester."

"We haven't any proof, Matthew," said the Doctor. "And listen, if what you suspect is true, it's going to be a very serious matter for all the people in the circus. Please don't say anything of your suspicions for the present, will you? There is no need to get the showfolk excited until we really know. Now, will you please saddle up a horse quietly and go into Manchester for me? See Mr. Bellamy and ask him if he knows anything of what has become of Blossom. Get back here and bring me word as soon as you can, will you?"

"All right," said Matthew, turning to go. "But I don't think Mr. Bellamy'll know any more of where our manager's gone than what you do."

Jip, after listening to this conversation, slipped away and joined the other animals in the Doctor's own wagon.

"Fellows," he said, shaking the wet off himself, "Alexander Blossom has skidaddled."

"Good heavens!" cried Too-Too. "With the money?"

"Yes, with the money—drat him!" growled Jip. "And there was enough coming to the Doctor to keep us in comfort for the rest of our days."

"I knew it!" groaned Dab-Dab, throwing out her wings in despair. "I told the Doctor not to trust him. I guessed him to be a fishy customer from the start. Now he's wallowing in luxury while we scrape and pinch to pay the bills he left behind."

"Oh, what does it matter?" cried Gub-Gub. "So much the better if he's gone. Now we'll have a real circus—the Dolittle

Circus—which the animals have always hoped for. Good riddance to Blossom—the crook! I'm glad he's gone."

"What you *don't* know," said Dab-Dab, turning on the pig severely, "would fill a library. How is the Doctor to run a circus without a penny in his pocket? How is he going to pay wages—ground rent? How is he going to feed the animals and himself? It costs pounds and pounds a day to keep a circus going, you pudding, you! And look at the rain— coming down as though it never meant to stop! And the whole show just standing here and not a soul coming to see it! And the payroll of dozens of men mounting higher every minute. *'Glad* he's gone!'—you—you sausage!"

After Matthew had gone the Doctor remained within the shelter of Blossom's deserted wagon, thoughtfully watching the rain splatter into the muddy puddles outside. Presently he sat down on an old packing case and lit his pipe. From time to time he took out his watch and looked at it, frowning.

After half an hour had gone by he saw Hercules, dressed in ordinary clothes, approaching across the enclosure. He was running to avoid the rain. Reaching the wagon, he sprang within, and then shook his wet overcoat outside the doorway.

"I hear the boss has skipped," he said. "Is it true?"

"I have no idea," said the Doctor. "He is late in returning from Manchester. But something may have detained him."

"Well, I hope he comes soon," said Hercules. "He owes me a week's wages. And I need it."

The strong man sat down, and he and the Doctor fell to chatting about weather and weather signs.

Not many minutes later along came Hop the clown, with his dog, Swizzle. Evil news travels fast. He, too, had heard a rumor that Blossom had deserted the circus. The Doctor

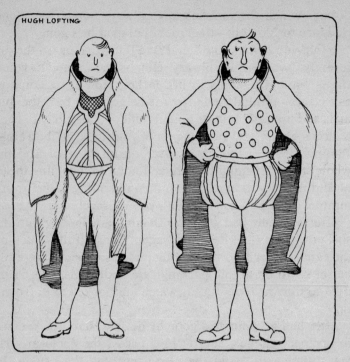

HUGH LOFTING

"The Pinto brothers arrived"

tried again to excuse the ringmaster and insisted that he be
not suspected till proof was obtained.

Then, rather awkwardly and without much interest, the
conversation continued about the weather.

Next, the Pinto brothers, trapeze artists, arrived with
mackintoshes thrown over their gawdy tights. They also
wanted to know where Blossom was and why they hadn't
received the pay that they had been promised would be
given them this morning. The Doctor, growing more and
more distressed, hoping Blossom would turn up any

minute, began to find it hard to keep the talk on any other subject but the mysterious disappearance of the manager.

At last the foreman of the tent riggers joined the circle.

"It looks rummy to me," he said when he had been told all there was to be told—"I got three children and a wife to keep. 'Ow are they going to live if I don't get no wages? My missus ain't got enough food in the wagon for another meal."

"Yes," said one of the Pinto brothers. "And we got a new baby in my family. If Blossom's running off with the money we ought to let the police know."

"But we have no proof he is running off," said the Doctor. "He may arrive any minute."

"And he may not, Doctor," Hercules put in. "If he is a queer one, by the time you get your proof he'll be in China, maybe—where nobody can get at him. It's nearly six now. The Pintos are right. What are we standing around here for, guessing and wondering? At least we ought to send somebody into Manchester to find out what we can."

"I have sent somebody in," said the Doctor. "Matthew Mugg, my assistant, has gone."

"Humph!" said one of the acrobats. "So you got kind of suspicious yourself, Doctor, eh? What time did you send him?"

The Doctor looked at his watch again.

"About four hours ago," said he.

"Time to get there and back," grunted Hercules. " 'E couldn't find no trace of 'im, I'll warrant. Boys, it looks to me like we was ditched, all right. . . . Lord! I wish I had 'im here. I'd make Mr. Blossom look like the last rose of summer."

And the strong man's hamlike hands went through the action of twisting the top off something.

"But 'e's left an awful lot of property behind," said the tent rigger. "I don't yet understand what made 'im skip at this stage of the game."

"What e' left behind—besides unpaid bills," said Hercules, "ain't nothing compared with what 'e took with 'im. 'Eaven only knows what 'e got from Bellamy for the Doctor's show —biggest takings this outfit ever saw. And all 'e give us was excuses—kept puttin' off payin' us for some fake reason or other—for three weeks back. I reckon 'e 'ad it in 'is mind to clear out all the time—'ad it planned as soon as 'e saw a big haul in sight."

"Well, what are we going to do?" asked Hop.

"Yes, that's the question," said the Pintos. "What are we going to do now?"

"We got to find another manager," said Hercules. "Someone to take over the outfit and get us out of this hole."

· The Fifth Chapter ·

THE DOCTOR BECOMES
MANAGER OF THE CIRCUS

IT was curious to see how, as soon as the strong man spoke of a new manager, all the eyes of the little crowd gathered in the wagon turned upon John Dolittle.

"Doctor," said Hercules, "it looks to me like you'd got to be the new boss. And if anybody was to ask me, I'll say you'd make a pretty good one. How about it, boys?"

"Aye! Aye!" they all cried. "The Doc's the man."

"That being the case," said Hercules, "in the name of the staff of the greatest show on earth, I present you, Doctor, with the circus of the late lamented Alexander Blossom. From now on, with us, your word is law."

"But—good heavens!" the Doctor stammered. "I don't know anything about circus management, and, besides, I—"

"Oh, yes, you do," Hercules broke in. "Wasn't it your act with Beppo that made the big week at Bridgeton? And wasn't it you what got the circus brought to Manchester? Why, bless me, you can talk to the bloomin' animals! We ain't worried. Meself, I've a kind of an idea we'll make more money under you than ever we made—or lost—under Blossom. You go ahead and manage."

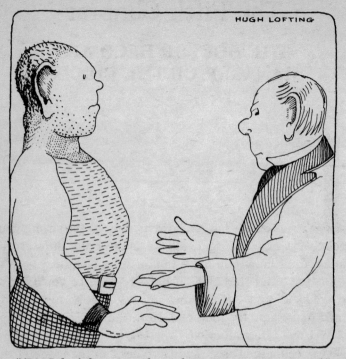

HUGH LOFTING

" 'But I don't know anything about circus management!' "

"Yes," said Hop. "That's right, Doctor. Lord only knows what's going to happen to us if you don't. We're in the soup —dead broke. And you're the one to pull us out."

For a full minute the Doctor did not answer—just sat, thinking, on his packing case. At last he looked around at the miserable waiting group and said:

"Very well. I had not intended going into this business for long when I started. But I certainly can't get out of it now— not only on your account, but on account of my own animals and my responsibility to them. For I, too, am—er— dead broke. If you want me to manage for you, I'll try it. But

I'm going to do it a little differently from Blossom's way. I'm going to run the circus on a cooperative basis—that is, instead of wages, we will all take our share of the money made, after expenses are paid. That means that when business is bad you will get very little—may even have to pay a little; and when business is good you will do well. Also, I claim the right to dismiss anyone from the circus without notice at any moment."

"That's the idea!" said Hercules. "That's the way a circus should be run—everybody partners in the business, but one man boss."

"But listen," said the Doctor. "For the beginning it's going to be hard work and very little money. We haven't got a cent in hand, and until the rain stops we shan't make a penny. What's worse, we will probably run into debt for a while—supposing, even, that we can get anybody to give us supplies on credit. Are you willing?"

"You bet we are!" . . . "We're with you, Doc!" . . . "Nobody's going to grumble!" . . . "You're the right boss!" they cried. And immediately the appearance of the whole crowd had changed from miserable gloom to hopeful smiles and enthusiasm.

In the midst of this arrived Matthew Mugg, with Mr. Bellamy himself.

"I'm terrible sorry to hear of this," said Mr. Bellamy, addressing the Doctor. "I gave that scoundrel Blossom two thousand pounds. He has cleared out with the whole lot, it seems—even left tradespeople unpaid in the city. It was their coming to me that first told me of his crookedness; and then your Mr. Mugg arrived. I've put the police on Blossom's trail, but I don't think there's the least chance of their catching him. You had better come back to Manchester, and

I will give you space at the Amphitheater park until you have made enough to carry on."

"Hooray!" yelled Hop. "And, look, the rain has stopped! Our luck has changed. Hooray for the Dolittle Circus."

"Pardon me!" said a small, polite voice from the door. "Is Doctor Dolittle here?"

Everyone turned; and there stood a small man in the entrance. Behind him the sun was now shining brightly.

"I am John Dolittle," said the Doctor.

"How do you do," said the little man. "I have been sent on a special mission by a firm of theatrical producers. I am instructed to make you an offer. They wish you to bring your troupe to London next month—if you have not been already booked."

"Hah!" cried Hercules. "What did I tell you, boys? First minute he's manager he gets an offer from Manchester and another from London. Three cheers for the Doctor!"

It was a day of great rejoicing for both the animals and the people of the circus when the Doctor took over the management. As soon as the news got around the enclosure, tent riggers, stableboys, performers—everybody, in fact, who was part of the establishment—came to the Doctor to congratulate him and to say how glad they were to be under his direction. With the stopping of the rain a general cheerfulness and bustle began. And the very first thing done was the taking down of the Blossom's Mammoth Circus sign over the main entrance and erecting in its place the Dolittle Circus—a more modest title, but one which was to become far greater and better known than Blossom's had ever been.

Mr. Bellamy was very kind. Realizing that the Doctor and everyone had been left practically penniless, he offered to help the new management with loans of money or in any other way he could. However, John Dolittle was most

"Putting up the new sign"

anxious to avoid getting the circus further into debt than it already was, and all he asked of Mr. Bellamy was to visit some of the tradespeople of this town with him and ask them to give him credit, to trust him for a while. Mr. Bellamy was, of course, very well known for miles and miles around Manchester. And the local corn dealer, grocer, butcher, and the rest were perfectly willing, when he asked them, to give the Doctor provisions and to wait for their money till the circus had made enough to pay its bills.

· The Sixth Chapter ·

MATTHEW MUGG, ASSISTANT MANAGER

ANOTHER member of the staff, besides Too-Too the accountant, to be more than usually occupied in the first days of the Dolittle Circus was Dab-Dab, the housekeeper.

"You know," said she to Too-Too and Jip one night, "all this looks very nice—and I certainly don't want to be a killjoy—but I wish we had someone else besides the Doctor to take care of the business end of things. He is fine where working out of new animal shows is concerned. As a stage manager no one could be better. But I know what's going to happen: all the other partners, Hercules and Hop and the Pintos and the rest, are going to get rich; and the Doctor is going to stay poor. Why, only last night he was talking about sending the opossum back to Virginia. He wants to climb trees, it seems—in the moonlight—and we haven't got the right kind of trees or moonlight here. I told him the moon in England is just as good as it is in Virginia. But he says it isn't—not green enough. Heaven only knows how much his ticket to America would cost. Yet I'm certain that as soon as the Doctor has the price of it he'll send him. He spoke of the lion and the leopard, too—says the big hunting animals should never be kept in confinement. I do wish we had some other man as well—somebody with good business sense—who could keep an eye on the Doctor's schemes."

"I quite agree with you," said Jip. "But I have great hopes of Matthew Mugg, myself. He isn't nearly such a fool as he looks."

"He's a very kind fellow," Swizzle put in. "Almost every time he meets me or Toby he pulls a bone or something out of his pocket and gives it to us."

"Oh, yes," said Jip. "That used to be his profession—cat's-meat man, you know. He has a good heart. And I think, Dab-Dab, you'll find he has a pretty good business head, too. It was he who arranged about the next three towns we're going to. The Doctor didn't know how to book the circus ahead or where to go next or anything about touring a circus around the country. He consulted Matthew. And Mugg went off at once to the next town and found out when the fair week was usually held and arranged for fodder supply and renting a show ground and everything. And he's just crazy about the circus business. I've often heard him boasting to Gypsies and the like along the road that he's the partner of John Dolittle, M.D.—the famous showman. He knows how to advertise, too—and that's important in this game. It was Matthew who got the Doctor to have those big posters printed. I hear they're already stuck up in every street in Tilmouth, our next town. Yes, I'm quite hopeful about Matthew. He's a good man."

The Dolittle Circus was an entirely new kind of circus. Now the Doctor proceeded to bring about the reforms and changes that he had so often wished for in the day of Blossom's management.

Certainly the average circus-going public had never seen anything like his show before. For one thing, John Dolittle insisted on the strictest politeness from all attendants. For another, he would allow no form of misrepresentation, as he called it. Ordinarily, circus folk had often been accustomed to say that their shows were "the greatest on earth," that their animals were "the only ones in captivity"—or something similarly extravagant and exaggerated.

This the Doctor would not permit. He said he wanted everything advertised just as it was, in order that the public should not be misled or cheated into paying to see something that they didn't see. To this, at the beginning, Matthew Mugg objected. He said you could never get a good crowd unless you "played it up big." But he soon found that the Doctor was right. When the people got to realize that whatever was promised in the Dolittle advertisements would be actually provided, the new circus earned a reputation for honesty that brought people in a way that nothing else would.

Another thing that worried Matthew was the Doctor's insistence on providing tea, free, for the public.

"Why, Doctor," he said, "you'll be ruined! You can't serve tea for thousands of people without charging them for it. This ain't a hotel—or a Widows and Orphans Home!"

"Matthew," said the Doctor, "the people who come to visit my show come long distances—with babies to carry. Afternoon tea is a nice custom. I hate to go without it myself. It won't cost so much when we buy the tea and sugar by the hundredweight. Theodosia can make it."

So afternoon tea for all visitors became an institution. And shortly after, another one was added: that of free packets of peppermints for the children. And what the Doctor prophesied came true. In one town where the Dolittle

"Free packets of peppermints for the children"

Circus crossed paths with another, a much bigger show, the Doctor's concern did twice the business that the other one did because the people knew that they'd be given tea and treated honestly and politely.

· The Seventh Chapter ·

THE DOLITTLE CIRCUS

IT was six weeks before the show was due to appear in London. The first town to be visited on the way there was Tilmouth. And it was here that the Doctor once more got put in prison—but only for one night. This is how it came about:

The animals, as I have said, were, if anything, even more pleased to exchange Blossom for the Doctor as a boss than were the human performers. And one of the first things that John Dolittle did, as soon as a little extra money was made, was to go around and ask all the animals if they had any complaints to make. Of course, there were plenty. To begin with, nearly every creature in the menagerie wanted his den repainted. So the Doctor had all the cages done over, each in the colors that its owner preferred.

Not long after the Doctor had had the menagerie done up, he received another complaint. This, indeed, was one that he had often heard before. The lion and the leopard were weary of confinement. They longed to get out of their narrow cages and stretch their legs in freedom.

"Well, you know," said John Dolittle, "myself, I don't

approve of keeping you shut up at all. If I had my way I'd ship you back to Africa and let you go free in the jungle. But the trouble is the money. However, as soon as I get enough together I will attend to it."

"If we could only get out a few minutes each day," said the lion, looking wistfully over the Doctor's shoulder toward the rolling hills of the countryside, "it wouldn't be so bad."

"No," said the leopard, "that would make life bearable. Oh, I'm so sick of the four walls of this wretched box!"

The tone of the leopard's voice was so pathetic and the lion's face so sad the Doctor felt that something just had to be done right away.

"Look here," he said, "if I let you out for a run every evening, would you promise me something?"

"Anything," said the two together.

"Would you come back at the end of half an hour? Honestly?"

"We would."

"And would you promise solemnly not to eat any people?"

"On our word of honor."

"All right," said the Doctor. "Then every evening after the show is over I'll open your cages and you can run free for half an hour."

So this, too, like the afternoon tea and the children's peppermints, became a custom of the Dolittle Circus. The menagerie animals were put upon their honor and allowed to run free every evening, provided they came back of their own accord. It worked surprisingly well for quite a while. The show people soon realized that the animals were acting up to their promise and could be trusted not to molest anyone. And even Theodosia got used to the idea of meeting a lion or a leopard roaming through the enclosure after dark on his way back to his den when his evening run was over.

"It is quite proper," said the Doctor. "I don't know why I didn't think of it before. They work all day, the same as we do—being on show. They deserve a little freedom and play-time at night."

Of course, the animals, when they went beyond the circus fence, were careful to keep out of the way of people because they didn't want to scare them—and people didn't interest them anyway. They were, in fact, heartily sick of them, having them gazing and staring in at the cages all day. But one evening when the circus had moved to a new town a rather serious thing happened. Matthew came rushing to the Doctor's wagon about ten o'clock and said, "Governor, the lion hasn't come back! I went around to lock up just now and found the cage empty. And it's more than an hour since I let him out."

"Good heavens!" cried the Doctor, jumping up and dashing off toward the menagerie with Matthew at his heels, "I wonder what's wrong. He certainly wouldn't have run away after giving me his promise. I hope no accident has happened to him."

On reaching the menagerie the Doctor went to the leopard's cage and asked him if he knew where the lion was.

"I think he must have gotten lost, Doctor," said the leopard. "We started out together and went for a stroll across that moor to the eastward. But it was new country to us. We came to a stream and couldn't get across. He went up stream and I went down, looking for a shallow place where we could get over to the other side. I had no luck. The stream got wider and deeper the farther I went along the bank. Then I heard the church clock strike and I realized it was time to be getting back. I expected to find the lion here when I got home. But he wasn't."

"You didn't meet any people?" the Doctor asked.

"Not a soul," said the leopard. "I passed a farm, but I went around it to avoid scaring anyone. He'll find his way back. Don't worry."

The Doctor stayed up all that night, waiting for the lion to return. He even went out into the country and hunted along the stream that the leopard had spoken of. But no trace of the missing animal could he find.

Morning came and still no lion. And the Doctor was very worried. However, the opening of the circus kept his mind occupied. The people came thronging in and good business claimed everyone's attention.

At teatime, as was his custom, John Dolittle acted as host to his visitors, and Theodosia was kept running back and forth waiting on the many little tables crowded with holiday-makers in their Sunday clothes.

Suddenly, just as the Doctor was passing among the tables to offer a lady a dish of cakes, he spied Mr. Lion strolling into the circus through the main gate. At the moment everybody was busy eating and drinking, and the Doctor hoped that the lion, who was quietly making for the menagerie, would reach his den before he was seen by the guests. But, alas! a party, a farmer and his family, coming out of the side show, ran right into the lion before he got to the menagerie door. There was a scream from the farmer's wife, who grabbed her children and ran. The farmer threw his walking stick at the lion and also ran. Then for a couple of minutes pandemonium reigned. Women shrieked, tables were overturned, and finally some stupid person in the crowd fired a gun. The poor lion, thoroughly frightened, turned about and ran for his life.

The excitement now partly died down, but the people were far too upset to stay and enjoy the circus any further, and very soon they all went off home and the enclosure was deserted.

So Mr. Lion, after his brief reappearance, was again missing; and the Doctor feared that now, terrified at his reception, he would be harder to find than ever.

John Dolittle was arranging search parties to go out and hunt when two policemen came to the circus and put him under arrest. He was charged, they told him, with keeping wild animals at large and endangering the public. Furthermore, the lion, it seemed, had broken into a chicken yard and eaten all the chickens. As the Doctor was marched through the town to the jail the owner of the chickens followed him, calling him names and telling him how much he owed him.

The Doctor spent the night in prison. But in the meantime the lion had taken refuge in the cellar of a bakery, and neither the baker nor anybody else dared go down to him. Everybody in the house was scared to go to bed. Messages were sent to the circus to send someone to take the lion away. But the wily Matthew Mugg, although he knew the lion was easily handled by those who knew him, told the people that the Doctor was the only one who dared go near him, and they better hurry up and let him out of jail if they wanted the lion taken away.

So early the next morning they came and set the Doctor free. Then he went down into the cellar and talked to the lion.

"I'm fearfully sorry, Doctor," said he, "but I lost my way out on that moor. I wandered around all over the place. And it wasn't until the next day that I found my own tracks and made my way back to the circus. I tried to slip into the menagerie without being seen. But when that fool started firing a gun I got scared and ran for it."

"But the chickens?" said the Doctor. "I thought you promised me not to molest anything when you were out?"

"I promised only not to eat people," said the lion. "I had to eat something. I was starved to death after wandering around that moor all night. How much are they charging you for the chickens?"

"One pound, ten shillings, and sixpence," said the Doctor. "Eleven at half a crown apiece."

"It's highway robbery," said the lion. "They were the toughest old things I ever tasted. And anyway, I ate only nine."

"Well, in the future," said the Doctor, "I think I had better accompany you on your walks."

Then he led the lion home. And the terrified townsfolk watched through the cracks of doors as the dread animal strolled down the street at John Dolittle's heels as meek and quiet as a lamb.

And now that the Doctor could give the animals the kind of consideration he wished, he really enjoyed the life himself a good deal. And poor Dab-Dab began to feel that her chance of getting him away from it, back to his own life at Puddleby, grew dimmer and more distant every day.

John Dolittle's chief occupation is his spare time was, as I have told you, thinking out new and interesting animal shows. And in doing this he always kept the children particularly in mind as an audience, and designed his plays and entertainments more for them than for the grown-ups. The success of the talking horse and *The Puddleby Pantomime* showed him that his knowledge of animal languages could be put to great use here. The snakes that he had bought from Fatima, for example, were later trained by him to give

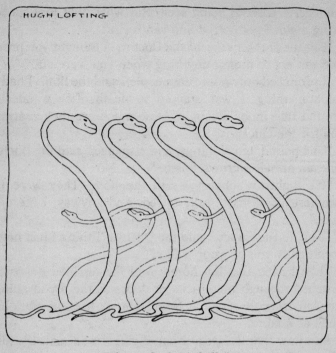

HUGH LOFTING

"The snakes' quadrille"

a little show of their own. Instead of a snake-charmer's tent
with a stupid fat woman in it, pretending to be something
that she wasn't, the Dolittle Circus had a sideshow where
the snakes gave their own performance, entirely unaided by
any person. To the tune of a music box they danced a very
peculiar but graceful sort of dance. It was something like a
mixture between a quadrille and a game of cat's cradle. On
a little stage of their own they glided about on their tails in
time to the music, bowing to their partners, doing the grand
chain, looping into knots with one another, drilling like

soldiers, and doing a hundred fascinating things that people had never seen snakes do before.

Indeed, as time went on, the Dolittle Circus's animal side-shows were almost without exception run independently by the animals themselves. There were a great number of them and each one was descriptive of that particular animal's special quality. The snakes' entertainment, for instance, was designed to show off their gracefulness for, in John Dolittle's opinion, the snake was the most graceful creature in the world. The elephant, on the other hand, did feats of strength instead of silly balancing tricks for which he wasn't suited.

"You don't want people in an animal performance," the Doctor said to Matthew one day. "Hercules and Hop and the acrobats, they're different. Those are shows given by people, where the human performers are the whole thing. But what's the sense in seeing a stupid man in uniform driving a lion through hoops with a whip? People seem to think that animals have no ideas to express. If they're left to themselves they can give much better shows on their own, once they're told what kind of things amuse a human audience—especially in the funny shows. The animal sense of humor is far superior to the human. But people are too stupid to see the funniness of things that animals do to amuse one another. And in most cases I have to bring them down to our level—to have them make their style of jokes rather—er—crude and broad. Otherwise people mightn't understand them at all."

And so, you see, the Dolittle Circus was indeed quite different from any other. The Doctor's kind and hospitable treatment of all who came to see his show made it more like a sort of family gathering than a strictly business matter.

There were no rules, or hardly any. And if little boys

wanted to see "behind the scenes" or to go into the elephant's stall and pet him, they were personally conducted wherever they wished to go. This alone gave the circus a quality quite individual. And whenever the wagon train moved on its way, the children would follow it for miles along the road and for weeks after would talk of nothing but when it would come back again to visit their town. For children everywhere were beginning to regard the Dolittle Circus as something peculiarly their own.

· About the Author ·

HUGH LOFTING was born in Maidenhead, England, in 1886 and was educated at home with his brothers and sister until he was eight. He studied engineering in London and at the Massachusetts Institute of Technology. After his marriage in 1912 he settled in the United States.

During World War One he left his job as a civil engineer, was commissioned a lieutenant in the Irish Guards, and found that writing illustrated letters to his children eased the strain of war. "There seemed to be very little to write to youngsters from the front; the news was either too horrible or too dull. One thing that kept forcing itself more and more upon my attention was the very considerable part the animals were playing in the war. That was the beginning of an idea: an eccentric country physician with a bent for natural history and a great love of pets. . . ."

These letters became *The Story of Doctor Dolittle*, published in 1920. Children all over the world have read this book and the eleven that followed, for they have been translated into almost every language. *The Voyages of Doctor Dolittle* won the Newbery Medal in 1923. Drawing from the twelve *Doctor Dolittle* volumes, Hugh Lofting's sister-in-law, Olga Fricker, later compiled *Doctor Dolittle: A Treasury*, which was published by Dell in 1986 as a Yearling Classic.

Hugh Lofting died in 1947 at his home in Topanga, California.